# TRIP OF THE DEAD

## BY ANGELA MISRI

**DCB**

Canada Council
for the Arts

Conseil des Arts
du Canada

ONTARIO ARTS COUNCIL
CONSEIL DES ARTS DE L'ONTARIO
an Ontario government agency
un organisme du gouvernement de l'Ontario

ONTARIO | ONTARIO
CREATES | CRÉATIF

Canadian    Patrimoine
Heritage    canadien

Canadä

The publisher gratefully acknowledges the support of the Canada Council
for the Arts and the Ontario Arts Council for its publishing program.
We acknowledge the financial support of the Government of Canada through
the Canada Book Fund (CBF) for our publishing activities, and the
Government of Ontario through Ontario Creates, an agency of the Ontario
Ministry of Culture, and the Ontario Book Publishing Tax Credit Program.

LIBRARY AND ARCHIVES CANADA CATALOGUING IN PUBLICATION

Title: Trip of the dead / Angela Misri.
Names: Misri, Angela, author.
Identifiers: Canadiana (print) 20200340867 | Canadiana (ebook) 2020034093X
ISBN 9781770865969 (softcover) | ISBN 9781770865976 (HTML)
Classification: LCC PS8626.I824 T75 2021 | DDC jC813/.6—dc23

United States Library of Congress Control Number: 9781770865969

Cover art: Nick Craine
Interior text design and racoon silhouette: tannicegdesigns.ca
Manufactured by Friesens in Altona, Manitoba in February 2021.

Printed and bound in Canada.

· DCB Young Readers
AN IMPRINT OF CORMORANT BOOKS INC.
260 Spadina Avenue, Suite 502, Toronto, ON  M5T 2E4
www.dcbyoungreaders.com
www.cormorantbooks.com

*For my sister, Anita,*
*my first choice in a fight against*
*the zombie apocalypse.*

# CHAPTER ONE

There's a man over there wearing my tail.

Well, not *my* tail, literally. My tail is still securely attached to my rump. I'm running my paws over it right now, just to be sure.

"Don't look at him," Ginger says, seeing what I'm staring at. Ginger's my best friend, a former alley cat with the style sense of one of those picture-perfect cats in one of those glossy magazines that we'd use to line our burrows behind the garbage bins in the city. It's a weird mix of personality traits packaged up in a slim orange cat with paws that look like slouchy white socks, but somehow, Ginger owns it.

Problem is, I'm not listening.

I can't tear my eyes away from the black and gray striped tail adorning the man's hat. It's not as sleek as mine, but then again, it's not being stroked the way mine is right now.

It's the first sign of another raccoon I've seen in months and it's so *not* the way I'd like this to have gone.

Every night I've gone out looking for more of my kind, searching high and low, from garbage pile to hollow tree. You might think that sounds easy. Fun even.

It might be.

If not for the zombies.

Dead humans in varying states of decay roam this land ready to pounce on anything that moves. They've taken over the top of the food chain, and raccoons and every other living thing do their best to avoid them.

The days of living in neighborhoods full of humans who helpfully walked their extra food out to convenient bins where we could sample it like a buffet were long gone. In the days before, my small gaze of raccoons lived in a large maple tree that we shared with four elderly chipmunks and seven squirrels from three different generations of the same family. I never really found out why a family of raccoons was called a gaze, but my den mother always said it was better than "a herd" or even worse, "a litter." Ew. Imagine being named for a box where you pooped.

But it was my brother who was the first to notice the change in our human neighbors — and of course, he noticed because of the food. First the humans just seemed to be spending more time in their houses with the doors locked. They seemed to throw out less food, and when they did it was sparse and tasteless. Fruits and vegetables all but disappeared to be replaced with mostly empty tin trays of frozen lasagnas and pot pies and curries. Those were my favorite, and I ate them even when my siblings purposefully put them under the garden hose or kicked dirt in them. Then those silvery trays disappeared from the garbage bins as well. No humans came out. They stopped walking their dogs and letting their cats out. And if they did come outside, the humans were armed. Out in the maple tree we started to hear from birds and other animals about a new predator stalking the streets — the undead human. Other raccoons we knew from the wider 'hood started to disappear and chipmunks and mice and many more. By the time my gaze disappeared, we were the last of our kind left for at least ten blocks in each direction. And then it was just me and the ancient chipmunks. And then, one morning I woke up and they were gone too. I started thinking I was the last raccoon on Earth. If not for the birds, I might have thought I was the last animal on Earth. And if not for Pickles and Ginger saving my life, I might not even be here at all.

So, my nightly searches for others of my kind are careful and stealthy, two traits I'm not exactly known for. They're also total fails. We've found cats, dogs, birds, and even an injured deer, but not one raccoon. The voice in my head tells me I'm the last raccoon on

Earth. It's an annoying voice, that doubt. Sounds a bit like a snake hissing its negativity into my ear with its long, forked tongue. I've never met a snake, but I guess if you were making a list of animals I don't want to meet, snakes would be up near the top. Number one would be zombies.

"Do you think he's staying?" I ask Ginger, watching as the humans of our compound flock around the stranger.

"I don't know," Ginger answers, his own tail flicking back and forth quickly, betraying how badly he wants to satisfy his feline curiosity.

"Ooof!" I say, expelling all the air from my lungs as Emmy barrels into us. For a smallish hamster, Emmy has this uncanny ability to inflict more damage than her size should allow. Thankfully, her berserker-like aggression is very effective against zombies.

She growls at the newcomer, sounding more like a panther than a hamster. I drop my tail and start stroking her instead. She puts up with it, something she never would have allowed when I first met her.

"Emmy, stay with Trip," Ginger says. "I'm gonna find out what's up."

As usual, I'm being handed off to a more capable mammal, in this case, a hamster about a quarter my size. Ginger scampers off to the front entrance where the humans are gathered. It's really just a large wooden gate wrapped in barbed wire. The stranger had to walk around the wooden spikes that form a perimeter around the camp, but the spikes are there to fend off zombies, not live humans with dead raccoons on their heads.

I climb up and onto the raised platform, Emmy at my side, and we watch Ginger weave and wind himself around the humans' legs.

There's a lot of courage crammed into the small body of a cat; they're like those backpacks with so many pockets you forget where you put things. I learned that months ago, following a cat named Pickles on her quest to find her pet, Connor. She didn't let anything stop her, not zombies, mad opossums, zealot cats, or greedy chipmunks. Did I mention the zombies? Yeah, they still freak me out.

"I heard there was trouble," says Wally, walking down the gangplank that links this raised platform we're sitting on to our home, The Menagerie. As always, the senior cat is followed by his squadron, whom he called the 4077th (which he explained as referring to an old television show about humans and war ... I didn't really understand). Ranging in age from 3 to 6 months, the 4077th are an excitable bunch of kittens of many colors and fur densities. Most had been rescued by humans and our own small fellowship, but not a few had been born within the safety of this compound and had never been outside into the real world. Lucky mammals.

Sonar, a particularly bouncy recruit, is hopping from

one paw to the other behind Wally's wide gray body.
Either she has information she's dying to share or she's
in desperate need of a litter box.

"Sir! Sir!" the small black cat finally calls, her patience
exhausted. "I can report that at thirteen hundred hours,
a dead raccoon was reported entering the compound!"

Wally's thick eyebrows shoot up and into his bangs.

"Not a zombie," I say quickly. "Not even a whole
raccoon, Wally, just a tail."

I turn away from the squadron, throwing back over
my shoulder, "And you've got your hours wrong, Corporal. It's after six in the evening."

Wally shakes his head as he says, "Corporal Sonar,
take the squad down to check on the repairs to the east
wall. I'll meet you there shortly."

I listen to them tumble down the stairs in a hissing,
hurried heap.

"It must be a shock, Trip," Wally says, sitting down
next to me, "to see your kind paraded around like a
trophy on a human's head, but I saw many such displays
before the apocalypse."

"Before the apocalypse, there were more raccoons
than you could shake a stick at," I reply. "And believe
me, I know. A lot of sticks were shaken at me. Though
nothing compared to …"

We both look out over the fence that borders our compound to the forest that surrounds us. We can see a few

zombies roaming in the trees, searching for live things to eat, their movements jerky and clumsy, not unlike myself when compared to the graceful cats I live with.

Since we had found Pickles' pet, Connor, our ragtag fellowship had been lovingly incorporated into this human community. They built us The Menagerie, a sort of tree house offshoot with a large central room and three entrances: one that leads directly to the humans' living quarters, a small hole in the ceiling that Pal uses to fly in and out and this smaller one that leads out and into the compound. Pickles and her partner Hannah live in a small room off the corner of The Menagerie, and Pal has a perch in the opposite corner above Emmy's burrow — a pile of shredded cardboard and fluff I had helped her gather.

In the very center of The Menagerie is a metal fire pit on wheels, really just a pile of warmed stones that the humans keep a fire burning underneath. That's where I sleep. Just another bump on a log. Nothing special for Trip — after all, I'm a raccoon, and raccoons live in trash and eat garbage.

All around the fire pit are pillows and blankets, so this is where I wander down to, leaving Wally on the platform. I bury myself in a cocoon of warm blankets. Trying to forget how very alone I am. Trying not to think about the ghost of a raccoon who drifted into my life today.

# CHAPTER TWO

"Hey Trip!" says Pallas, poking at me with the tip of his wing. "Wanna go out hunting?"

Pal is a small burrowing owl with soft brown feathers and the deepest voice you can imagine. Think of Darth Vader's voice coming out of the body of an ewok and you get the picture.

"Nah," I reply, sinking deeper into the warm pile I've made for myself.

Pal pokes his beak into my plastic bag, where I store all my precious findings. There's not much in there right now — a few elastics, a broken doll, a half-filled water bottle, and a small, battered fanny pack I found in the mud a few days ago.

"Maybe later?" Pal hoots hopefully, as he takes off through the raised sky tunnel that connects his perch to the dark sky outside.

All around me, the non-nocturnal animals slumber.

Ginger is snoring on his back, his white paws moving, even in sleep. Emmy is grinding her teeth, like always. Wally is surrounded by his squadron. Every time he tries to shift away, seven small furry bundles sleepily follow, rolling and purring their way back to him.

I close my eyes again, willing my brain to stop thinking.

# CHAPTER THREE

"Trip, you haven't eaten in days," Pickles says. She means well, but her voice is grating on me. I know we're the same age — about three years old — but sometimes she acts like she's old enough to be a den mother. I hate it when she tries to bully me.

"I ate. Last night, while you were sleeping," I lie.

Pickles looks at Hannah, who shrugs. They were happily ensconced in their love nest in the corner of The Menagerie. I know they can neither confirm nor deny my claim. I pull a blanket up and over my head. It's too much of a bother to discuss anyway.

# CHAPTER FOUR

I can hear them whispering about me up in Pal's perch. I don't care. I really don't.

"He needs food."

"He needs more than that."

"Let's start with the basics, shall we, Ginger?"

"No, Ginger's right. We need to deal with the under-lying problem."

"Oh, Saber save us from psycho-babble please ..."

"He's depressed, Wally!"

"He's fine."

"NOT FINE!" bellows Emmy, effectively silencing everyone. Thankfully.

I start to drift off again. The warmth of the fire pit and my burrow of blankets comforting me. Lulling me away from the anxious voices of my friends above.

# CHAPTER FIVE

Small gifts have started to appear around The Menagerie. A container of half-eaten Cheetos shows up in my plastic bag. A trail of jerky appears, leading to the door that takes us outside into the compound. I'm sure they are meant to tempt me out of my cocoon. They don't.

Last night the 4077th surrounded me instead of Wally, and their warm purring bodies should have comforted me — I love a good cuddle — but they didn't.

The Menagerie is empty now. Quiet. Like a tomb. Which feels appropriate.

I shift my position. It feels like my tail has fallen asleep. I twist and turn, trying to free it, but I can't feel it, so I can't get it loose.

"Great galloping garburators!" I curse, throwing off my blanket for the first time in days. I back away from my pile of pillows, taking hold of my tail with both hands and shaking it, trying to wake it up.

For a second, I feel nothing. It's like a dead thing in my hands and I start to freak out.

"Asleep?" asks Emmy, scaring me.

"Gah!" I squawk, dropping my tail in fright.

Emmy responds by jumping on my tail with all four of her paws, and I feel that, the pins-and-needles feeling filling my tail.

"My tail fell asleep," I say, my eyes drifting away from the hamster and to my safe cocoon a few inviting steps away.

Emmy is a plain brown hamster with the heart of a Viking, forged in the fires of this zombie apocalypse. She lost her two best friends to zombies, a pair of Great Danes named Vance and Ralph, and it took her a long time to recover from that. I'm not entirely sure she has, actually. But where I still feel lost and alone and cowardly, she deals with her pain with violence and aggression, which seems to work for her. This is why I'm totally shocked when she gets up on her hind paws and tries to wrap her tiny arms around me in a hug. The hug goes on for longer than I thought she could stand still, but ends with a vintage Emmy command:

"Let's go find that dead raccoon."

# CHAPTER SIX

"So, what do we know?" Pickles asks as we sit gathered around our small fire pit. Pickles is our *de facto* leader, a calico cat with a smattering of freckles across her pink nose. A cutie pie and the exact opposite of her girlfriend, Hannah, who's an elegant Abyssinian with limbs as long as my tail.

"Pickles," calls her young charge as he toddles into The Menagerie, closely followed by his mother. Connor is Pickles' pet, and the whole family was under the charge of Pickles' housemate, Wally. Unfortunately, the male of the human family was lost in the apocalypse, making Wally's assignment all the more important. Or so he tells us. Often.

"Give us a minute," Pickles says as she and Wally leave our circle to meet their pets at the door.

"The stranger is called 'Duke,' and he comes from

another camp across a river," Ginger offers, picking at his teeth with a sharp claw.

"Bad guys?" demands Emmy as she orbits our fire pit at a steady clip. This hamster is terrible at sitting still.

Ginger shrugs. "So far, our humans seem suspicious but curious, so I'd say ... neutral."

I wince, and Hannah notices, her long golden tail wrapping around me protectively. "He can't be all that good if he's walking around with that hat on his head."

Her empathy surprises me. I'm used to being run over by the more assertive animals in our group. Oh sure, they listen to me, but I always feel like they do it out of love, not because they value what I say. At least it's better than before zombie times when we were chased away and hissed at by most every animal in the neighborhood — from human to hamster. My gaze never seemed to take their negativity to heart, but I worked hard to change hearts and minds. I remember this one time when my gaze was arguing with some tough alley cats behind a restaurant about some fantastic-smelling leftovers. I was holding on to my brother's leg so that he wouldn't hurl himself at the sharp-clawed felines, while also keeping an eye on the kitchen door, lest we all get chased away by the humans who would hear this ruckus and deny all of us this meal. Between growls on both sides, I managed to point out that most of the

food in the garbage was tainted with fruits and vegetables that cats had no interest in. The biggest cat stuck
his head into the bin and agreed with my assessment.
That gave me an idea, and ideas make me feel brave.
Before my siblings ruined my progress, I suggested that
just we two, the top cat and I, would divide up the food
equally, with more veggies for us and more meat for
them. My gaze made fun of my peaceful solution, but
we all ate so well that we slept for a full day. I learned
something about myself that day. I'm no fighter. I'm
a negotiator.

"Let's be realistic, Hannah," Pal says. He's holding
a small stone and sharpening my claws with it. "Your
own pet, Rosa, wears a cow-skin coat and has a feather-
filled pillow."

Hannah has a quick and clever tongue, and she looks
ready to argue, but then she notices Pickles motioning
her over with her tail.

"Sorry, be right back," Hannah says, joining Wally
and Pickles at the doorway with their pets.

"What else?" asks Emmy on her next pass.

"He's heading back to his camp tomorrow," says Ginger, distracted by all the signals coming off the other cats'
tails and whiskers. Something about the way their tails
are flicking in unison, I think. Feline languages are very
subtle, and though I've been practicing with Ginger, I'm
still not fluent. Whatever is going on, surely they can put

it off for five minutes of their nine lives to focus on the possible extinction of my race.

"Good riddance," Emmy growls.

"Other paw, Trip," Pal says, his wing extended. I switch paws so he can sharpen the claws on this one, a kind effort to relax me.

Wally, Hannah, and Pickles finally turn away from their humans, but Connor runs back in to give Pickles an extra hug, and then they're gone. I stuff down my jealousy like a bag of marshmallows and ask, "What was that about?"

"We're to take on an important new assignment," Wally announces, rubbing at the bronze star on his collar proudly.

Pickles looks too dizzy to speak, so it's Hannah who says, "Connor's mother is very pregnant. With twins, they think."

"Twins?" Ginger repeats.

"Twins," Pickles whispers, sitting down heavily, a grin slowly spreading underneath her whiskers.

# CHAPTER SEVEN

I can't wait to see the back of this stranger.

Sitting up on the guard tower level with Ginger at my side, I glare down at the man. He's still wearing that raccoon-icidal hat. I wonder if he's noticed me. Noticed how a raccoon tail should look. Attached to a live raccoon.

The humans of our camp stand around in a tense circle. Sarah and Uma are traveling to his camp with him. Something about trade opportunities, which I know a little about, though most of my trading was with other raccoons, chipmunks, and squirrels. Chipmunks are ruthless traders.

Sarah is one of my favorite humans. She always leaves the lid to the small garbage open for me, and she can't stop giggling when I wash my paws under the water barrel. Uma saved me from a pack of zombies once. I wasn't paying attention as I picked berries next to a stream and froze in place when they came out of the bushes. That's kind of my thing when it comes to zombies — freeze and hope for the best. It's not a great strategy, I know. Only Uma's quick response saved me from being a tasty dead human treat that day. She's a tough old bird with an eagle's beak-shaped nose and eyes that are just as sharp.

I don't want either of them to go with this stranger.

Wally and his squadron walk by at ground level, the kittens falling out of formation every few steps.

The old gray cat stops suddenly, causing the kittens to bump into each other like somebody spilled a basket of multicolored yarn balls. If yarn hissed.

Usually, Wally would turn into his drill sergeant best, barking orders at this chaotic infraction, but something the humans are saying has his gray ears moving like mini satellites on the top of his head.

Sonar races around the hissing squad, trying to reorganize them before Wally notices.

"What's up?" I ask Ginger, who is watching Wally's tail and whiskers like I watch a human eating a drumstick — just waiting on the tips of my toes for them to be done with it so I can get my paws on it before one of the other scavengers.

Before Ginger can answer, Wally glances our way and bowls over his newly organized squad.

I leap down into the dirt, tripping over my own feet,

but managing to meet him halfway. "What?" I demand.

"Other raccoons!" he says as he skids to a stop. "Duke says there are entire families of raccoons at his camp."

"No freaking way," I reply immediately, pointing at the man's hat in disgust. "No self-respecting raccoon could live alongside a mammal who wears them as a hat!"

Wally shakes his head. "It sounds more like they're POWs than members of the community."

"POWs?"

"Prisoners of war," Wally explains with a grimace.

My stomach twists painfully, reminding me of the days before I found Pickles and Ginger in that apartment. When dodging zombies and eagles felt like I was on the losing side of a war I didn't start. I don't think I've had a secure night's sleep since the dead humans appeared.

"I have to help them," I whisper, shocking my furry friend. I'm a little shocked myself. I'm no adventurer! That's Pickles' job. Or Ginger's. Or ... really, anyone but me. But once the words are out of my mouth, I find I can't take them back. And the belt that's been squeezing my heart since Duke arrived starts to loosen.

"I have to go help them," I say, hoping I sound more confident than I feel and feeling that belt loosen a notch more. I need to find my own kind. It'll help me figure out my place in this new, crazy world. Maybe I'll feel like there's a place for me in this other camp. Or maybe

I'll find a new gaze to be a part of. It would be wonderful to be a part of something again.

"Are you daft?" Wally asks as all these thoughts run through my head.

Duke, Sarah, and Uma shoulder their packs and start to walk towards the east gate tower, where Ginger still sits, so I follow them.

"Tell everyone I'll be back as soon as I can," I say to Wally, waving at Ginger as we pass under his guard post.

He leaps down. "Where the Saber do you think you're going?"

"With Duke."

"What?"

"His camp has raccoons," Wally explains, between ordering around his squad, who are seconds away from being trod on by the humans escorting this group out of the compound.

"His camp kidnaps raccoons," I correct for Ginger's benefit, grabbing a black kitten by the tail before he can be trampled.

"I can't stop him," Wally says. "And I can't abandon my pet in her imminent delivery. It's my mission."

I stop for a second to hand Wally the kitten, and he grabs it by the nape of the neck and tosses it to safety.

"I will be careful, old friend," I say to Wally, trying to

head-butt him as cats do, something Ginger has been instructing me on.

I'm not sure how successful my head-butt was, but Wally sits down at the gate, sparks of frustration coming off his whiskers in the form of static. His duty holds him here. He gathers the 4077th around him with a loud command and all eight cats salute us smartly.

"Are you sure about this?" asks Ginger as he gives a truly terrible salute that makes Wally wince.

"Not at all," I reply, unhelpfully, as the gate starts to close behind us.

"Then I guess I'm coming too," Ginger says.

I smile, feeling better with my best friend at my side.

"Now, are we traveling *with* the humans, or just following them to this other camp?" he asks.

I automatically look behind us for Wally or Pickles to answer, only then realizing that he's actually asking me. Golden garbage piles, he thinks *I'm* leading this mission?

"Uh, I dunno, what do you think?" I hedge, pulling at my whiskers.

He blinks in that annoying feline way. "Depends. Do you trust them?"

I look at the dead raccoon tail bouncing at the end of Duke's hat and shake my head immediately. I may not be sure of much, but I will never ever trust that human.

Before I can answer aloud, Sarah looks back and, seeing us, says, "Hey, you guys better stay close to camp.

A herd of zombies passed this way a few hours ago."

Duke glances back and does a double take. "Are you talking to the animals?"

Sarah gives him a look that shuts him up and I love her for it. She may not be a youngling like Connor, who can still understand us, but she at least tries to communicate with us.

I poke Ginger, and we drift to the left, giving the impression that we're taking her advice.

"Trees?" Ginger suggests.

"Trees," I agree, climbing after my feline friend, keeping the humans in sight. It's a good thing I got that manicure from Pal when I did, because otherwise, I wouldn't be able to climb as fast as Ginger.

Speaking of the owl, a loud thump signals Pal's arrival on the scene, as he smacks face-first into the trunk of a tree. He backs up on shaky legs and I leap onto the branch to grab him, tucking him under my arm and swinging to the next branch so we don't lose the humans.

"Trip," Pal says from under my arm. "You can't just leave like this."

"Says who?" I reply, swatting the first drops of rain I feel.

Pal wiggles free to fly onto the next tree branch and narrowly misses the bough, fluttering back up to try again. I get the sense that Pal didn't get a lot of flight instruction as an owlet, because his approach to landing on a branch is to fly above it, clamp down his wings to his sides and drop like a stone onto his target, just hoping for the best. It works about half the time.

"Pickles says —"

"Pickles isn't here," I reply, cutting Pal off. "And that isn't a cat tail that man is wearing."

"We could wait for Pickles and Wally," Ginger starts to say, but I interrupt him too, stopping to put my paws on my hips, the rain flattening my fur to my body and making me cold as well as grumpy. I spent too many years before this apocalypse being bullied and I'm sick of it. I'm sick of all of this.

"If we wait, that guy might outfit his whole camp in the latest raccoon-tail fashion," I hiss at the owl and cat on the branch ahead of me. "You two are lucky. There are cats everywhere, and Pal, owls seem to be in every second hollow tree. Remember that nest of newborn owls we found two weeks ago? They're under a heat lamp being fed human baby formula back at camp. Your species will survive this apocalypse. Raccoons might not! We're in danger from the dead humans *and* the live ones it looks like, so if you don't mind …"

"Look out!" yells Sarah from below.

I whip around to see a zombie crunching through the underbrush, straight towards the humans, and I lose my balance.

I hit every single branch on my way down to the soggy ground.

"Trip?"

"I'm fine," I grumble as Ginger lands gracefully on the forest floor beside me. The zombie is a huge bear of a former man, with arms the size of lampposts, but Sarah and Uma dodge around him nimbly, even as Duke swings at it with a bat. The impact of bat against bone is thunderously loud and Duke is knocked back onto the ground.

Ginger's ears are flat against his head, his back arched, his muscles coiled to leap into action should the zombie turn our way. I'm doing everything I can not to run screaming back to our camp, my paws are dug into the soft earth, holding me in place. What made me think I could do this? The snake-like voice in my head immediately kicks in. Calling me a coward. Telling me to turn tail and run.

Sarah is so calm in the face of this monster that I feel all the more guilty for my prostrate panicked position. She carefully measures the distance as the zombie bends towards Duke and takes off its head with one slice of her large sword.

Uma wipes at her forehead. "Good one, Sarah."

The rain is coming down harder now, making a palpable sound as it hits the ground all around us in a staccato rhythm.

Sarah extends a hand to Duke, who is still lying on the ground, gaping up at her.

"Helluva job," he agrees, taking her hand and standing up. And then he touches at his head. "Hey! Where'd my hat go?"

Sure enough, the tail of my kin is no longer hiding Duke's very bald pink head.

"Let's wait out this rain," Uma says, ignoring Duke, who has stooped to search for his hat in the mud at their feet. "Do you see a cave over that rise, Sarah?"

"I do," Sarah replies, squinting in that direction. "Let's go."

Pal comes in for one of his rolling landings, his claws clutching something dark and heavy. He swoops low, and as usual, misjudges how close the ground is, hits it and rolls three times before coming to a stop at our feet. In his right claw is the striped tail of a raccoon attached to a hat.

I smile for the first time in a week, and we follow the humans to find our own shelter near their cave.

# CHAPTER EIGHT

Pal and I share more than just our locomotive clumsiness. We're also both nocturnal, so while Ginger curls into a ball to sleep away the night in the hollow of a tree I found for us, Pal and I talk.

"Trip, we have no idea what we'll find at that camp," Pal says, rocking on the tree stump just outside the hollow.

"Is that supposed to convince me to give up?" I ask, looking at the owl incredulously. "I'm more scared than you, I promise. My knees haven't stopped shaking since we left and I haven't eaten a bite, and you know that's weird for me. How can I ignore the first sign of other raccoons we've had since ... before?"

"Before" holds special meaning since dead humans started gobbling up the top of the food chain and working their way down. Everything earlier than their appearance is "before."

Pal tilts his head side to side unnervingly. I'm never entirely sure his head is connected to his body the way he can rotate it like that.

"You were part of a gaze," he says finally. "Before."

"I was," I reply, remembering smiling masked faces, distinctive smells, both good and bad. Racket smelled like cupcakes and whiskey, and Barrow smelled like fancy coffee grounds. The kind you find outside one of those hipster cafés along with gluten-free this and vegan that. Blech. "We weren't all related by blood, and they weren't that nice to me to be honest, but we were the same. I never had to explain anything to any of them. They knew. I knew I had a place in my gaze."

"But I thought they left you. As my family did. After," Pal says, with a soft hoot that I think is meant to soften the words.

I notice that I'm pulling at my whiskers, and stop myself with an effort before answering, "I don't know what happened. I fell asleep in the morning as usual, in my hollow, and when I woke up, all the other raccoons were gone, and the zombies were pacing under my tree."

When he tilts his head again, I sigh. "Look, I'm not trying to pretend it can be like it was before, but I want to be a part of something again."

"Aren't you a part of us?" he hoots. "You and Ginger and Emmy and Pickles and Hannah and Wally, and even those mad kittens in the 4077th? Why isn't that enough for you?"

"Because you guys don't need me! You're all brave and smart and can fight zombies, for the love of garbage! Maybe if I find other raccoons, I'll feel less useless," I say, tears coming to my eyes. "I don't know why that's important, but it is."

"We do need you," he says with a shake of his head. "But I understand what it is to feel alone. It's how I felt before Pickles and Emmy found me. I just didn't have a word for it."

I gulp and find all I can do is nod.

He wraps a feathered wing around me, starting to cry as well. "You are never alone, Trip. Never again. I will go with you and find your kin."

We're both crying now, and that's never a good scene, so I pull myself together. "Hey, starlight's wasting! Go find us some food, wouldya? My stomach is lonely."

He hoots in response, brushing away tears, and he flies off to find some breakfast.

He's a dot against the moon when I decide to perform some kind of service for the animal who died and became a hat.

I dig a shallow hole with my paws in the wet earth, the smell of decomposition and earth and rain comforting me. I sniff at the tail, catching bare hints of strawberry jam under the more human smells, and then carefully tuck the tail into the hole. I pile the dirt back on top and raise my hands out to the rain, watching the dirt wash away as I try to think of something to say.

Wally would probably want some kind of military service involving loud guns.

Pickles would no doubt quote her favorite dead English poet.

Emmy would light the place on fire and screech at the top of her lungs like she was in Valhamster.

"All I can think of to say is that I'm sorry you're gone," I say finally. "And that I hope your belly was full when whatever happened … happened."

A squeak from the darkness pulls my attention from the grave.

"Pal?" I call, wondering how I had missed his distinctive landing.

No answer. I turn away with a shrug, scanning the area for some flowers I can place on the grave when I hear a cry of pain.

Alarmed now, I pad over to the tree where I hear and see Ginger snoring softly. I climb the trunk up to the lowest branch and look all around for the source of the sound. I'm squinting into the rainy darkness, cursing my nearsightedness when I see something small and black. What is that? Is that … a tail?

My life is becoming a series of strange quests involving tails.

I bound back down the tree to where a very wet, very small, black tail sticks out of a knothole of a skinny log. It's shaking badly — the tail, not the log — though whether that's from fear or cold rain, I can't tell.

The log is so narrow I can either stick in my snout in the hollow or press one eye against the opening. I choose the eye and recognize the owner of the little black tail.

"Corporal Sonar, what are you doing out here?"

The kitten looks miserable, but manages a sniffle. "My claw is stuck, Mr. Trip. Please help. I can't get loose no matter what I do."

She seems to have a familiar black strap wrapped twice around her torso, but I push down my questions, switching positions and sticking my arm as far as it will go into the log. I'm in all the way up to my shoulder and I still can't reach her.

"Can't ... quite ..."

I switch back to my eye in the opening to say, "Okay, don't panic, we'll figure this out." I am not sure who I am trying to reassure, her or me, but I look around for something that might help me.

"I wish I had my plastic bag," I whisper to no one in particular. I usually find something useful in there from my gatherings. Should I wake Ginger? I don't think he'd fit in this log, it's tiny. Just the size of Sonar or Emmy.

Maybe I should send Pal for help. I raise my face to the pouring sky, looking for the owl. I need help!

"Mr. Trip?" Sonar calls from inside the log.

"Just Trip. Okay, Sonar?" I reply, still looking at the sky, hoping for someone to tell me what to do.

"I'm sorry to bother you, but ... I'm getting awfully wet," she says, the panic seeping into her voice. Cats and water. Pickles says it's number one on their list of worst enemies, followed by cucumbers, rats, #4, and dogs. I'm not supposed to ask about #4. Maybe it's skinny hollow logs.

"Try not to think about the water," I say instead, sticking my eye in the hollow again to see the shivering feline shake water off the paws that aren't stuck. She manages to pull her tail out of the knothole above her, but now water is streaming in from above her as well.

"Och! Tha's a problem."

I leap backwards at this new voice, landing awkwardly on my rump.

"Who ... said that?" I ask, wiping rain out of my eyes and turning around in a semi-circle from my semi-prone position.

"Me," says the voice, and as I squint, I can barely make out a small mammal with a very spiky hairstyle sitting atop Sonar's watery wooden prison.

"Mr. Trip?" calls the cat.

"Mr. Trip?" repeats the well-coifed animal. "That's a proper name if I e'er heard one that is."

"Hold on, Sonar," I say, picking myself up with as much dignity as a muddy raccoon can manage.

"Och, I dinnae think that's likely," replies our spiky stranger, sticking his eye into the knothole Sonar's tail had been sticking out of moments before. "This here log is fillin' up with rainwater faster'n a good pint at the local pub!"

This animal has such a strong accent that I'm only catching about half of his words, but Sonar seems to understand everything, because she wails in response, her tone moving from worry to full on freak-out.

"You'd better get her outta there," the animal advises in an infuriatingly calm voice.

"Thanks for the advice," I say sarcastically, running around the log to the other end. It's no wider from this side, but I have an idea. I lift the whole log above my head.

"Sonar," I yell, rain and strain making it hard to talk. "Is the water draining out?"

"Y— yes ... I think so," she answers, the terror in her voice a terrible thing to hear.

"Just how long d'ye think you can hold this log up?" the world's most annoying hairdo asks from right above my head. His added weight can't be much, he's about the size of the kitten I'm trying to save, but the weight of his sarcasm is killing me.

"Get off!" I growl through my teeth, trying to do my best Emmy impression. "If you can't help, at least get out of the way!" I shake the log, trying to dislodge him, but he's a solid bump on this log.

"Och! You cannae unstick me laddie," he says, actually grinning down at me and my shaking arms. "Don't ye know anything about hedgehogs?"

"Hedgehogs?" wails Sonar.

I'd never even heard of a hedgehog before, but something he said makes me ask, "You're good at sticking to things?"

"Oh, I am. Well known for it. Why, I remember one time down at the races in Belfast ..."

"That's too bad," I interrupt him.

"Too bad?" the hedgehog repeats, getting up on his tiny legs to look down at me with beady eyes. "Why's it too bad?"

"Because what we need is an UNsticker. Not a sticker," I reply, huffing now, my breath coming out in short bursts of steam. "Someone who is an expert in UNsticking. Oh, never mind, what I need is my friend Ginger. Could you go down into that hollow —"

"What? That lanky orange cat that walks around on his tippy toes?" the hedgehog says, turning to spit for emphasis. "Don't be daft, laddie. He wouldna know how to unwind a keg from a pile let alone how to detach a cat from lumber!"

I gape at him, because his words make about as much sense as a locked compost bin, but before I can say anything he climbs down onto my head and into the log. Sonar squeaks in surprise, but I hear him trying to calm her down.

"Now lassie, I'm not here to hurt you. Just move aside a wee bit so I can see what you've gone and done to yourself. What's this bag 'ere? Nevermind, I see what the problem is. Now, just do what I do ..."

I wait, flexing my arms for several heartbeats until I can wait no longer.

"Sonar?" I call.

Silence answers me, and I shake the rain from my ears, straining to hear something. That doubting voice in my mind switches to paranoia and I nearly lose my grip on the log. Had this all been an elaborate trick? Were these hedgehogs kitten-eaters? Ninja kitten-eaters?!

"Corporal! Answer me!"

"Present!" says a tiny voice at my feet.

This time I *do* drop the log and narrowly miss crushing the very kitten I'd been trying to save.

# CHAPTER NINE

"You're going back," Ginger says again, standing over the smaller kitten imperiously, giving an awesome impression of angry Wally.

I kind of love watching a bully fail to intimidate. It's something I always dreamed of doing back when I was being pushed around by every animal in my neighborhood. I'd often come up with the perfect comeback a half-hour after I'd been pushed out of my favorite garbage can or the day after being chased up the wrong tree by some mean dogs. In this case, my best friend is acting like a bully, so he deserves to be stood up to by a cat half his size. As usual, a tiny mammal is showing more bravery than I ever have.

"Oh no, I'm not," declares Sonar, glaring up at the orange cat, her black fur matted with mud and slime. It was probably killing Ginger to stand so close to a cat that was that filthy and didn't care about it. "General

Wally sent me out here with this fanny pack thingy for Mr. Trip and told me to help him on his mission."

The fanny pack was one of my found items from my precious plastic bag, and it's filled with berries and nuts and a few chocolates. Sonar carried it all the way out here for me, by herself. I'm wearing the black strap around my torso from shoulder to hip rather than around my waist.

"Well, now we have the funny pack, so you can go home," Ginger says.

"*Fanny* pack. And I still have to help Mr. Trip," Sonar says, sitting back on her haunches and crossing her arms.

"This is ridiculous," Ginger says, stomping off dramatically. If you can stomp on your tiptoes. Because that's how Ginger does it.

"I'll say," says the hedgehog. "That little cat's got more spunk in one paw than I've seen outta the lot o' you."

"Who asked you?" yells Ginger over his shoulder, out of sight but by no means out of hearing range.

"Who is he again?" hoots Pal, directing the question at me, but pointing at the hedgehog.

"Says his name is Malone," I reply, my eyes on the humans, who are in the final stages of their morning routine. "And he talks more than three normal mammals combined. He says he's a hedgehog, whatever that is."

"Whatever that is? Och, laddie, the hedgehog is indigenous to Europe, Africa, and Asia, and there are a lot of different kinds. I, for example, am from the great *Erinaceus europaeus* family, and I can tell you, the import rates on a mammal such as myself ..."

"See what I mean?" I say, nodding at Pal, who is listening to the spiny little beast raptly.

"You can go back together," I say, getting to my feet, dusting off my paws, as the humans leave the cave. "There's no way they're inviting a hedgehog into The Menagerie without a proper introduction, so he'll need an escort."

"We're not leaving you," Pal says immediately, throwing a last apologetic glance at Malone. "I'll scout out which way the humans are heading next."

I climb the nearest tree trunk, and Ginger leaps from a branch to the one above me.

"So ye're just gonna leave us here?" the hedgehog yells up at us.

I look back down to see Sonar struggling to climb the tree trunk, a look of determination on her young face.

"Don't worry Mr. Trip," she grunts, whiskers trembling. "I can keep up."

Ginger rolls his eyes at me. "What do you want to do?"

Shrugging is a bad idea on skinny tree branches, which I discover, slipping right off the branch and into a thorny bush below.

"Ow!" I yell, feeling every scratch.

"Tch tch," says the hedgehog, sticking his long snout

into the bush without fear. "Tha's no way t'go berry picking laddie."

"I wasn't … oh never mind," I say, dragging myself out of the bush. "We'll stay at ground level for now. Pal can keep the humans in sight from the air."

And so, we walk. One orange tabby in the lead, a tiny muddy black kitten directly behind and a soggy raccoon wearing a battered fanny pack in step with a very talkative hedgehog.

"Reminds me of the time my sweet Arin got lost in a gorse bush," he says, shaking his head at the memory. "She was always losing her way, my Arin. Prettiest hedgehog you ever did see, but terrible sense of direction."

"Uh huh," I reply, not really listening, my eyes on Pal as he circles back towards us. I can tell he's tired by the way he's flapping. This was usually the time of the cycle when he and I would be fast asleep in The Menagerie. "Shouldn't you be getting back to her now?"

"Who?"

"Arin?"

"Och! I cannae do that now can I?" he replies with a shake of his head.

I'm scared to ask why because it may lead to another long-winded story from the old country, but I'm saved by Pal swooping low over our heads.

"River ahead," Pal calls from above us, before turning back to chase the humans.

"More water?" wails Sonar and then, remembering that she didn't want to be sent home, "I mean ... whatever ... more water ... no biggie."

I speed up my pace. I want to see just how much of a "biggie" this river is.

"Why, I remember this one night after she was out with her mates playing mahjong ..."

"What's mah ... muh ...," Sonar asks, struggling with the word.

"Mahjong? Och, marvelous game. I could teach it to you," Malone answers, speeding up his little legs to catch up with Sonar.

"You guys should hang out here and play," I say, passing them and catching up to Ginger to see the river. "We can pick you up on the way back from Duke's camp."

"Don't you think you're being a little hard on them?" Ginger says out of the corner of his mouth as we leave them a few steps behind.

I throw a glance over my shoulder. "Are you kidding me? You're the one who's bullying Sonar into going home."

"For her safety."

"Nowhere is safe right now," I say. "And that Malone character is a delay animal if I've ever met one."

Ginger snickers. "You know we used to say that about you, right?"

I can't argue with that. I've always suspected that the rest of this group looked upon me as the hanger-on.

"Sorry I couldn't be as useful as Emmy, or Wally, or Hannah," I say, unable to keep the hurt out of my voice.

"I was totally kidding, Trip. Besides, since when do we measure friendship by how useful someone is?" Ginger challenges me.

"Since the future of my species became a story of extinction," I reply.

I speed up even more, leaving Ginger behind. No one is taking this mission seriously. Sure, Pickles loses her human pet and everyone jumps on her quest, four paws in. Wally should be leading this rescue. I'm not qualified. I might be the last free raccoon on Earth and I'm hampered by baby cats, incomprehensible balls of needles and oh yeah, zombie attacks.

This time, they come right out of the water. Water sluices off their rotting bodies in slow motion as they drag themselves towards the shore. I'm running away before they step foot on dry land.

I careen around the corner and back into the forest, scooping Sonar up by the nape of her neck and yelling at Malone and Ginger through my teeth and her fur. "Run!"

Ginger climbs a tree at record speed and I follow him.

"Pass up Sonar!" he calls down from a branch.

I grab Sonar out of my mouth with one paw and push her up towards Ginger. He grips her by the nape and puts her down beside him where she clamps on with all claws, just like Wally taught her. Only then do I turn around to see one of the zombies is still groaning her way towards us.

My heart nearly stops when I see Malone in one of the zombie's hands, his spines sticking up through the flesh. He's sneezing his tiny nose off. Every time he sneezes, a wave of spines comes flying off of him in every direction.

The zombie can't seem to figure out what to do about the animal stuck to her hand. Twice she raises her hand to her mouth and twice comes away with spines in her face. They don't actually seem to hurt the dead human, but they don't allow her to eat the hedgehog.

"That's right ye evil blighter," Malone yells up at the zombie, following another sneeze, "take a mouthful o' that! I got plenty more where those came from!"

From my tree branch, I can see the other zombie has turned back towards the river, perhaps sighting our humans. I'm frozen in place on this branch. Someone has to save that hedgehog, but it can't be me. I can't move.

"We have to help Mr. Malone!" says Sonar, her back arched like the world's tiniest stegosaurus. "What do we do?"

"I don't know," I answer, heartily sick of being asked that and swearing to myself that I will never bug Wally or Pickles with that question in the future. Now we're all hanging over the branch, staring down at the frenzied display below, and trust me, it's crazy. Even the squirrels living in this tree come out to see what the fuss is about.

The zombie is waving her hand frantically trying to unstick the hedgehog from her appendage. The hedgehog is sneezing his spines off and using such foul language against his aggressor that Ginger wraps his tail over Sonar's ears.

"Pal, make sure we don't lose sight of the humans," I yell, seeing my owl friend fly by. I turn to the squirrels, who just dodged a volley of spines and are now shaking their tiny fists at Malone. Where did they come from? Ahh, their burrow is right there. That gives me an idea. "Hey you! I need to trade for some string. Now!"

Squirrels, like chipmunks, are avid traders. They love nothing more than hoarding useless stuff in their burrows and bartering back and forth loudly for the newest and shiniest bits. I love that about them.

"Huh?" says one.

"Yes! Trade!" says the smarter one, diving back into her house in the tree.

That unsticks my frozen limbs, and I scramble past the confused squirrel and stick my head in the hollow of the tree. "Anything?" I yell down, my voice echoing back at me.

It's black as licorice in here, but I can hear the scratchy sounds of someone digging through a pile of goodies. It's a reassuring sound I know well from when I too had a warm home in a tree.

"This!" announces the squirrel around a mouthful of purple sparkly shoelace. It's the prettiest thing I've seen in days. I grab it from her and run back out onto the branch.

"Malone!" I yell down, sure this isn't going to work, but just as sure I have to try.

The hedgehog looks decidedly greener than his usual gray and brown, from being shaken around like a broken toy.

"Grab this!" I say, throwing one end of the shoelace down towards the zombie's clenched spiked hand.

Malone reaches out to grab the shoelace, but misses as the zombie spins, still trying to shake off the spiny mammal.

"Hey!" yells Ginger from the branch above me, drawing the zombie's dead eyes up to meet mine. I freeze again. I can't even feel my paws let alone the shoelace I'm holding.

"Trip!" Ginger yells.

"Huh?"

"The shoelace!" Ginger says, hissing at the zombie as it careens toward us.

"Hurry Mr. Trip," squeaks Sonar.

For some reason, it's her voice that jerks me back into motion and I throw the shoelace again. This time, Malone manages to wrap a small pink hand around it just as the zombie hurls herself at the tree trunk with a tooth-jarring thud.

I, of course, fall right off the branch, but my weight pulls Malone free of the zombie with a surprised yelp. I'm holding on to the shoelace with both hands as Malone shoots up past me towards the branch I just exited. I look down, trying to see what brand of thorn I'll be pulling out of my rump when I jerk to a sudden stop.

Now I'm hanging in the air like a big round pendulum. I look up to see Malone has jammed the quills of his back into the tree branch and is giving me a truly maniacal thumbs-up. Wait, do hedgehogs have thumbs?

"Climb!" I hear Ginger hiss down at me, and I thank the Gods of the Garbage that someone else is giving orders again because that gets me going, climbing paw over paw back up the purple shoelace to my friends.

# CHAPTER TEN

The sun is beginning to set by the time the zombie loses interest in us. Enough time to negotiate a napping spot in the squirrel's home. We trade information about safe foraging spots to rent their little burrow for Pal and me to catch a few Zzzs. The cats curl up around us (because cats can sleep anywhere, anytime) and Malone insists on standing guard on the branch just outside the hollow.

I wake up first, being extra careful as I extricate myself from the pile of mammals. This burrow smells hauntingly like home. My home before. Hints of wood and moss mixed with nuts, pine, and sap. I know I'm remembering my life before with nostalgia. It wasn't all warm burrows and fair trades. There was a lot of risk being a raccoon in a big city full of humans who, for some reason, don't want to share their garbage. But at least I knew that game. The rules have changed so dramatically that I just can't keep up.

I tuck the purple shoelace carefully into my fanny pack and climb out and onto the branch. I hear Malone before I see him. He's sitting between the squirrels. Shockingly, the squirrels are hanging on his every word, listening to his tales of the olden days across the ocean, sharing nuts back and forth, dropping shells on the ground below where you can hear them skitter to a stop, scaring the bugs they land near.

I take a different route out of the tree, traveling from branch to branch to reach where the humans have made a small camp at the edge of the forest by the bank of the river. I walk out onto a leafy branch so that I'm hidden from the humans, but well within hearing distance of their conversation. There's no sign of either of the zombies we encountered, and I wonder if they wandered back into the water or were dispatched by Sarah and her handy sword.

"Here, eat something," says Sarah, holding out a piece of tofu jerky to Duke.

My stomach growls in response, and I dig into my fanny pack for a few berries to quiet it. Duke is standing with his hands on his hips, facing the river, but looks back over his shoulder with a grimace at Sarah's words. I look out over the river and my stomach turns from hungry to queasy. It's choppy, and based on the dark color, looks too deep to wade through. It's wide enough that the other side is a blurry landscape of green and gray.

Duke runs his hands over his non-existent hair, turning back to Sarah to say, "This is messed up. We should just go back to your camp."

"You give up too easily," Sarah replies, taking a bite of the jerky and swallowing it down with a swig of water from her bottle. My stomach growls again, returning to its normal setting of hunger over fear.

Duke paces back and forth in front of the little fire they've built.

"If there's a safe spot to cross, Uma will find it," Sarah says, taking another bite of jerky, and making a face. She throws it over her shoulder and into the woods, and I'm back down on the ground gobbling it down before she finishes her sentence. I can move like a cheetah when food is involved. And like a sloth wearing a blindfold the rest of the time.

"I just don't know what could have happened to the raft," Duke says, shaking his head.

"Describe it to me," Sarah says. "Again."

He sighs, but says, "There's this square raft. Super crude, but it worked."

Sarah nods, so he continues; we're both listening raptly.

"We tied a rope around this tree," he says, walking over to a large trunk and pointing at the wear marks. "And another rope across the river around another tree. Then each end of the rope was tied to the raft so that you can just tow yourself to the other side like a pulley."

"So, the raft is always on one side of the river or the other?" Sarah asks, looking out over the water.

"Yeah, but there's no rope and no raft," Duke says, flapping his arms dramatically like a turkey.

Sarah cracks her knuckles, something she does when she's thinking hard. Sometimes, when I return from my dinner hunt covered by the darkness of night, I will see someone sitting down at the big central bonfire in the center of our camp, and I will know it's Sarah by the sound of her cracking of her knuckles. And sometimes I will climb down and join her as she tends the bonfire, and she will smile at me and share whatever snack she has brought with her.

"But how did they do it the first time?" asks Sarah, pulling me out of my memories as I clean my whiskers of salty jerky residue.

"What do you mean?"

"The first time you set up your rope and pulley raft system," she says, "you had to get ropes around trees on either end of this river. So, how'd you get across the first time?"

"I don't know … I didn't set up the raft system …,"

Duke says, looking confused, but I think I know what she's talking about. You might not know this about me, but I'm an expert finder. I can find anything. Usually, what I find gets thrown into my plastic bag of goodies, and as a trade union of chipmunks can attest, that makes me one professional looking finder. I look around the trees, climbing a trunk to see better. I find what Sarah is looking for as she is explaining things to Duke for the second time. I climb a few branches and then shake them dramatically to get their attention.

"What the peanut butter are you up to, raccoon?!" a squeaky voice yells at me.

I look down to see a squirrel with a long flowing tail that belongs in a shampoo commercial. Seriously, it seems to have its own wind machine. Ginger would love it. The frown on the squirrel's face and the paw he's pointing at me are not as attractive.

"What?" I yell back, still trying to get Sarah's attention.

Sarah walks up and under the tree, pointing up. "There!"

"Gah!" the squirrel chirps, scurrying back to the safety of his hidey hole, tail and all.

"What?" Duke asks.

I fade further back into the foliage, repeating a mantra under my breath: "Don't fall out of the tree, don't fall out of the tree."

"The arrow," Sarah says excitedly. "The first time they

crossed, they shot an arrow attached to a rope and held on to it as they waded through the water to the other side."

Duke looks from the arrow to the river and then back again. "Are you kidding me?"

"Are you kidding me?" I whisper, realizing what Sarah is proposing, and what my latest find means to my quest. I never should have left the camp. I clasp my paws to my head and knock a bundle of nuts out of the tree with a crash.

"Are you kidding me?" shrieks the squirrel from his hidey hole, and I fall backwards out of the tree.

# CHAPTER ELEVEN

"I don't feel so good," says Ginger as I gobble down the mushrooms that Pal dug up from the forest for me. Look, we all deal with scary news differently. Don't judge. Pal and I just finished explaining the humans' plan to get across the river to our small group.

"That sketchy-looking bloke doesn't look so good either," Malone says, spitting for emphasis. "Reminds me of a dizzy camel I met once at a petting zoo. Why he …"

"Uma's trying again," Pal announces from the branch above us, and we all turn to look through the trees to see Uma pull her bowstring taut. She holds the arrow close to her cheek, her fingernails showing her inclination for biting them when she is stressed. And with zombies all around, it's a miracle she has nails at all. She releases the arrow and it flies across the river in an arc, the rope tied to the end marking its journey in a neon orange streak. Higher and higher until it starts its descent and then *thunk!* It plants itself in the trunk of a tree on the other side.

"Nice!" crows Sarah, offering a high five that Uma readily smacks, a huge grin across her lips.

"Yeah, nice," repeats Duke, looking far less excited.

Uma pulls carefully on the orange rope, and then a little more. "Feels pretty secure …"

"Only one way to find out for sure," Sarah says, taking the coil of rope and tying it around a thick tree trunk.

"This is crazy," Ginger says, his eyes wide, his whiskers vibrating.

I agree, but say nothing, stuffing the last of the foraged mushrooms into my mouth, watching every move Sarah makes.

She walks back toward the riverbank, tugging on the rope. "I'll go first," she offers.

"You sure?" asks Uma, tying her gray hair back in a ponytail.

"Yeah, I'm the smallest, I'll put the least strain on the rope," Sarah answers, pulling off her sneakers and stuffing them and her socks into her backpack. We're lined up at the edge of the forest. She steps out into the river, both hands gripping the rope that is strung across as she slowly walks further and further into the current.

"Take it slow," Uma suggests from the bank, her hands balled into fists. I'm pulling on my whiskers and even Malone has stopped talking as we all tensely watch Sarah's progress. She makes it in up to her knees, then her waist, and finally the water is up around her shoulders.

"Now I know I'm going to throw up," Ginger says, looking away. "Tell me when it's over."

"She's okay," I say, as much for myself as in support of Sarah.

That's when her blond head disappears under the water.

A collective gasp rises from our group, and Ginger grabs my tail, his face still turned away from the river. "What? WHAT?"

"Sarah!" Duke yells, grabbing hold of the rope.

Uma is frantically yanking off her shoes when Sarah pulls herself back up and out of the water, and I start breathing again, "She's okay; she slipped or something."

"Or the river got too deep," Malone says.

"She's through the worst of it," Sonar whispers, her paws reflexively massaging my tail. "Isn't she?"

"Yes," I reply, as Sarah's shoulders appear out of the water again. "She's coming up the other side."

Sure enough, a few anxious minutes later, Sarah emerges fully on the other side of the riverbank, shivering and wet, but very much alive. She bends over at the waist to catch her breath, spent, but at least she made it.

"Sarah?" Uma calls across the river.

"I'm okay," Sarah calls back, sounding as winded as she looks. "There's a spot in the middle there where the bottom drops out. Be careful."

She takes a few more breaths and then walks over to the arrow stuck in the tree trunk. It takes her a long time to untie the rope from the arrow's shaft with her shaking hands, but she does it. While she throws the rope all the way around the trunk and ties it securely, Uma stores her shoes in her backpack.

"You ready?" Uma prompts Duke, taking hold of the newly secured rope.

"Not really," Duke answers, but follows her into the river.

Pal does a looping pass over the humans' heads. "Who wants to catch him this time?" Ginger asks.

"I got 'im," says Malone, toddling out onto the sandy riverbank.

"No!" Sonar, Ginger, and I all yell at the same time.

"Oh, right," says Malone, running his paws over his spines with a giggle.

"I'll do it," Sonar says, bouncing out to stand near Malone. She sits back on her haunches and opens her arms wide as Pal comes in for his landing. He drifts down lower and lower and lands just in front of the small cat. I actually open my mouth to congratulate him when he trips forward and, tumbling beak over drumstick, bowls into her, narrowly missing the hedgehog.

"Sorry kid," Pal says, patting her awkwardly on her head. "Thought I had it that time."

"No problem, Mr. Pal," she replies, on her feet in a trice with a salute, Malone dusting her off. "Happy to be of service."

"They're still walking, but I'm pretty sure I know where they will stop for the night," Pal says, hopping over to talk to Ginger and me. "There's a small cabin a couple of hours away that Duke has been talking about."

"Okay, good," I say, rubbing my paws together and looking around for someone to lead us. "Then we just need to get across this river."

"Oh, that's all?" Malone repeats, spitting sharply into the river.

Ginger won't even get that close. He sits in a patch of sunlight he's found on the beach, his whiskers shivering in anticipation. But what he says just underlines that feline bravery I was telling you about before: "I'll go first."

He leaps straight up in the air and grabs the rope in his jaws. He hangs there for a minute, reaching up with his paws, trying to grasp the rope, but — lacking thumbs — he's unable to wrap his padded digits around it.

He drops to the ground, graceful in his failure. "Okay, so that didn't work."

I look down at my thumbs. "I guess I could try," I say,

hoping someone will disagree, and volunteer instead. No one does though. I slowly dip my paws into the river to clean them like a gymnast about to take to the uneven bars. Still no other volunteers. Golden garbage piles. I guess it's my turn.

I climb the tree the rope is attached to (there's no way I can leap straight up in the air like Ginger, best not to try) and grab the rope with both paws. Paw over paw, I make my way back to the beach. Now I'm dangling over my friends, the cord slightly dipping from my weight. I'm totally surprised I've made it this far, but I keep going. Now I'm over the shallow part of the river. I'm sweating like it's mid-August in a parked food truck, but I'm still moving forward. I can hear my friends cheering me on from the other side of the bank, behind me, and Pal swoops and comes in for a landing on the other beach ahead of me. I don't look back. I can't. But I do look down. And that's a mistake. The water below me looks as black as the bottom of a garbage bag.

"Don't stop!" Pal yells from the bank in front of me. He's so far away.

But I have stopped. I can't pull my eyes from the water. And I can't make my paws move forward.

As if that wasn't bad enough, now I'm swaying, the wind is picking up and really not helping the situation. I can feel the panic rising in my stomach like a rotten meal coming back to take its revenge on me.

"I'm going out to get him!" I hear Ginger yell from far behind me.

"Ye can't, laddie!" replies Malone's voice.

"Can raccoons swim?" asks Sonar.

That's a really good question. I've never tried. The doubting voice in my head doesn't think so. He's laughing at me. I stare at the water below. Do I want to try going forward or do I drop into the water below and try to swim? I look at the beach ahead and try to unclench my right paw. I put all my willpower into it. Move forward. MOVE. FORWARD.

"Trip!"

"Gah!" I say, and now I'm dangling by one paw, staring up at Pal, who is circling my position like a tiny vulture. I try to reach up and grab the rope again with my right paw, but I miss. I'm holding on with my left paw with everything I've got.

"I'm coming, Trip!" he yells, coming in for a landing on the rope.

"No, don't!" yells Ginger from the beach, seeing what the owl is doing, but Pal is my friend, and he thinks he can help. He slows down right above the rope and drops with all claws extended like he's landing on a branch. I wait to feel the claws dig into my remaining paw when he misses the rope as he undoubtedly would, but he misses so wildly that he drops past the rope, past my body, his eyes clamped shut.

"Pal," I whisper, as I watch his body drop like a stone into the water below.

I let go of the rope.

The water hits me like a door slamming in my face, cold, solid, unforgiving. I struggle to open my eyes under the water. I have to fight the overpowering urge to push to the surface; instead I turn around in a circle, looking for Pal. I see him immediately, his eyes still shut tight, tiny bubbles leaving his beak, his feathered arms wrapped protectively around himself. Somehow, I paddle over to him, I'm moving all my limbs, but they don't seem to have a unified plan. My lungs are burning by the time I get both arms around him and start kicking towards the surface of the water. We bob up and I suck in a gasping breath.

"Trip!"

I can't answer. The current pulls us down and I kick with everything I've got, breaking through the surface again. I squeeze Pal and he coughs spasmodically.

"Dog!"

I must have water in my ears because this time, I could have sworn I heard Ginger yell "Dog!"

I shake my head, my vision clearing as I realize what Ginger is yelling about.

"Log!" I sputter, coughing out water. I try to bob over to the log that seems to be floating upstream past us, but I don't want to unwrap either of my arms from the owl. I won't have the energy to find him again underwater. I am not taking the chance of losing him. I lean hard towards the flat part of the log and clamp on with my teeth. That's when I remember logs don't really have flat parts.

I hear someone ask, "What in tarnation?" and then we're airborne.

We hit the sand on the other side of the river and roll to a stop, my arms still tightly around Pal.

"Pal?" I ask, scared to open my eyes.

"Yeah?" he replies from my arms.

"Are we dead?"

"Don't think so."

"You don't know?"

"I've got my eyes closed," he admits.

"Open your eyes!"

"No! You open *your* eyes."

"Someone better open someone's eyes or I'm gonna smack you both into next Tuesday," says the voice of the log that tossed us ashore.

I open my eyes to see an animal with huge teeth standing over us and I have to swallow before I can speak again.

"Well?" she asks, slapping her large flat tail on the sand. It's the sound of that tail that puts it together for me: she's a beaver. No wonder she was swimming against the current.

I get to my feet and put Pal down next to me on the

ground. The owl tips over immediately, so I right him, and keep a paw on the top of his head while he uncrosses his eyes.

"Ma'am, I am so sorry for ... for ...," I start to say.

"For biting my behind?" the beaver offers, waggling dark brown eyebrows at me.

"I'd never ... I mean, I thought you were ...," I'm blubbering at this point. I look at her tail and realize, yes, I did bite her tail ... thinking it was ... a log. Classic Trip move.

"Trip!" Ginger yells from the other side of the river.

"Hold on to your fleas, cat! We're in the middle of a palaver here!" the large-toothed animal yells back, sending a glare his way. "You were saying, raccoon?"

The word *palaver* triggers the negotiator in me, and I stand up a little taller, water dripping off my body, and pooling at my feet. "I was apologizing for biting you. We were drowning and I panicked. I have no other excuse."

My words seem to surprise her, because she whistles between her teeth, "Is that so?"

"It is," I reply sincerely. "And we totally owe you our lives for ... flicking us to safety like you did."

Pal shakes his wings free of moisture, and tips over again. I right him again, trying to maintain a bit of professionalism in this negotiation.

The beaver smiles, or at least I think she does. Hard to tell with those two huge front teeth blocking all of her dentition. "Well, it just so happens I'm in need of some help."

I hesitate. I really need to keep up with Duke and Sarah and Uma, but looking back at my friends across the river, I know I can't do it alone. I can see the anxiousness on their faces even from this far away, and a plan starts to form in my head.

"I'm Trip, and this is Pallas," I say, Sonar's military parlance springing to mind. "How can we be of service?"

"You can call me Mrs. King," the beaver says with a nod. "My young'uns are the ones who need the help. They're too small to understand this new dangerous world we live in. I need to build them a stronger more defensive dam. And I need someone to help me."

I glance around. If there was a dam, we might have avoided all this dunking and drowning.

As if anticipating my question, the beaver says, "It's a ways downriver from here, but if you'll come with me, you'll see the problem."

Pal clears his throat, and as usual, his deep voice is a surprise coming out of such a tiny body, but he ignores the beaver's shocked look and says, "I'd think, based on our performance in the water, Mrs. King, that you should find more aquatic animals to help you ..."

"No, no," I say, grabbing the owl's beak to stop him from ruining my crazy strategy. "We can help. We're happy to help."

The beaver looks skeptical, so does the owl, and now they're both tilting their heads at me, so I stutter out, "We can watch your kits while you work, Mrs. King ... and we can ... teach them! Yes, we can teach them how to fight the zombies!"

"You?" she asks. "*You* know how to fight zombies?"

"Not me," I point across the river, "but those mammals are experts. That's why we're traveling with them. Those cats and that hedgehog. They can teach your kits. *If* we can get them across to this side of the river, that is."

Pal has recovered enough to fly ahead and check on the humans, so I'm standing alone on my side of the river, watching anxiously as Mrs. King glides back across towards me, Ginger standing on her flat tail, looking totally freaked out. If he were any stiffer, he'd tip right off Mrs. King's tail. Even his tail is standing straight up along with every orange hair on his body. It's sad because it's the best entrance I've ever seen him make. I can practically hear the theme music from the *Pirates of the Caribbean* playing.

Mrs. King is a smooth swimmer and delivers him from the opposite bank to the one where I stand waiting within minutes.

"Thank you," Ginger says through his clenched jaw as he tries to disembark from the tail without bending any of his appendages or getting wet. He fails at both, tiptoeing onto the sand and then immediately shaking his paws of the wetness.

She's on her way back to get Sonar and Malone before he whispers to me, "Never make me do that again."

"Sure, the beaver will probably sublet her dam and we can send Pal back and forth with messages to Pickles' camp," I say, nodding.

"Sarcasm is cruel this close to water," Ginger says, moving away from the shoreline to follow Mrs. King, who has begun leading us down the beach towards her dam. "I just mean we need a new way back across."

"Do you think we could walk back across your dam?" I ask the beaver, hopefully.

"Depends," she replies, waddling beside me, her tail moving in a slow rhythm. "My dam runs the full length of the river; it's not as wide down where we built it, but there are pieces missing that need attention for sure."

We walk for nearly a half hour before I realize that I may not be coming back. This might be a one-way trip for me, if I find what I'm looking for.

"Trip?"

"Hmm?" I say, brushing away the thought, like a cobweb covering the doorway.

"Sonar," Ginger says, pointing at the black kitten on the back of the beaver.

Against all feline instinct, Sonar is grinning from ear to ear, holding on to the tail with all four paws, as the wind ripples her long black fur. Beside her paddles the hedgehog, one paw holding the beaver's tail as he is pulled along.

"This is SOO cool!" she calls out as they glide to a stop in front of me.

"You are one weird cat," I say, wading into the water and picking her off the beaver's tail so she doesn't have to get wet.

The beaver puts her two paws to her mouth, letting out a sharp whistle.

We watch as tiny ripples appear in the water and grow as they get closer to us. Five small beavers surface, each fuzzier and more adorable than the last, and come up on the shore.

"Hetty, Olivia, Alec, Ruth, and Roger," Mrs. King says, brushing a piece of flotsam off one of the kits' shoulders. "These mammals are here to help us."

"I'm Ginger," Ginger says, stepping forward. "And that's Trip, and Sonar is the kitten …"

"*Corporal* Sonar," Sonar says, standing at attention and saluting the younger mammals, who mimic her in an adorable attempt to salute back. "And this is our friend Malone. He's a real hedgehog."

"Now, let me show you what I need," Mrs. King says, grabbing a small twig and scratching in the sand at our feet.

We divide into two teams: the mammals who can deal

with water, and the ones who consider water an evil supervillain bent on ending their species.

The sun is starting to set when I leave the beach, following Malone and Mrs. King, leaving the instructors and their students behind. Ginger is playing the part of drill sergeant and Sonar walks between the recruits, adjusting their tiny bodies.

"The first step is to not panic," I hear Ginger say to the kits, "because you're going to want to scramble and hide, but you need to have a plan."

Ha! Easier said than done my young mammals. Panicking is what I do best!

"I cannae help but notice, Mrs. King, that Mr. King is nowhere to be seen," Malone says to the beaver, as we follow her upstream to her dam. I'm nervous of leaving the cats behind with the kits, and I keep scanning the skies for Pal. I need confirmation that the humans are down for the night in that cottage, and that we have time to catch up to them. I'm also worried about being alone. I barely know this hedgehog and I just met this beaver. I wish Ginger were with me and Malone were back there helping Sonar.

"No," she answers, shaking her head at us. "We lost papa right at the start of this. He heard sounds and went out to see if it was hunters wandering a bit close to the dam, and never came back."

"Och, I'm sorry lass," Malone says.

Mrs. King nods. "We aren't the first to lose someone. The beaver family we know upstream of us lost all their kits to the dead humans. Every one of them." She throws a look over her shoulder at her tiny offspring on the beach.

"I can't imagine," I say, and I mean it. I may not have seen another live raccoon in months, but losing this new family of mine — Ginger, Pickles, Pal and everyone else — would be unimaginable. Heck, even Malone has poked his way into my heart.

"Here," she says, turning left, back towards the river. "You can see the problem, right?"

Even someone who doesn't engineer dams can see the problem. There's a moldering zombie stuck head-first in one end of the dam. He's less than half a zombie, but despite missing his lower torso, his arms are still moving, scrabbling at the logs and wood that hold his head in place.

"How in the world …?" Malone asks.

"Did he drift downstream and just get stuck?" I ask, pulling on my whiskers at the sight.

"No, he was trying to get in," Mrs. King answers, leading the way over top of her dam. We follow carefully, it feels barely strong enough to support my weight. "Scared the splinters out of us when we saw him stick his head in through the entrance there, so we ran out the exit.

"I dropped a log on him, but he was still pushing

through, so we dropped all the logs on him, took out our back wall."

"And now he's stuck," I say, looking down at the zombie and wondering how I can possibly help. You can't talk a zombie out of a dam. "He can't pull himself out and you can't shove him out from the inside."

She nods. "I'm just going to seal him in so that he can't get to us or do any more damage to the dam. The entrance is this way. It's underwater, but you can hold onto my tail, I'll pull you into the dam lickety-split."

I hate that plan.

"Wouldn't it be easier to kill him?" I ask, stalling.

"Kill him?"

"Yeah, you know," I make a swiping motion across my throat, "like really dead. Not zombie dead."

"You can kill these beasts?" she asks, incredulous.

"Oh, yes lassie," the hedgehog says, as if he's been dropping zombies left, right, and center. "Turns out even dead humans need their heads."

Pal swoops overhead and comes in for a rolling landing on the beach.

"They're halfway to the cabin, and they're already wiped, so they'll be staying the night for sure," Pal yells in a hoarse voice, looking so tired he can barely stand. "They've fought off two groups of zombies already."

"Galloping garburators," I curse, hoping Sarah and Uma survive. The raccoon-killing man, I couldn't care less about, but if he leads them to a horrible death, I will have even more to hold against the guy.

"Take a nap, Pal," I yell back at him. "I'll wake you in a few hours."

Pal nods, and heads to the nearest tree, looking for a burrow.

"Ready?" asks Mrs. King, sliding down the side of her dam and floating next to it expectantly.

I won't go into detail about our short journey from the river's surface down, down, into the inky darkness of the dam's underwater entrance. Actually, I can't go into detail because my eyes are closed the whole way, my paws clamped to Mrs. King's tail. Suffice to say that I kick Malone in the face in my desperate scramble from the water to the relative safety of the inner dam. I shake my fanny pack free of water and give myself a shake as well.

Things you may not know about the inside of a dam: they are surprisingly dry and cozy, like the inside of a burrow, but there's the constant sound of rushing water all around you. I think it would be a friendly place if there weren't a zombie head stuck in it. Not my style, but certainly a viable option in the midst of a zombie apocalypse.

They're dark places, but not pitch black, which makes sense, since they are underwater but not so deep in the river that sunlight can't still filter down. Beavers must have a better sense of sight than raccoons, because I bump into the walls of the dam following Mrs. King. I run my hands along the walls and learn something else; they are more than just wood. The beavers who built this dam used anything they could find to build it — plastic, wood, mud, and in at least one wall, what looks like an old rug.

"There he is," Mrs. King announces, pointing at the gruesome gnashing head. Most of the skin and hair is missing from this dead human, and it's not an improvement, I promise you. I actually turn away from the sight so I don't throw up and embarrass myself.

Malone opens his mouth and I raise my paw before he can speak. "Don't ask me what my plan is, please."

"But you have one?" Mrs. King asks.

I have the beginnings of one, but I nod as if I do this kind of thing all the time. "You're the only one who can fix your dam, Mrs. King, so if you gather whatever you need to repair this hole, we will take care of this interloper."

She glances from me to Malone, who nods, and then she glides back into the river. I wait until the ripples have disappeared from the surface of the dark water before turning to Malone.

"How sharp are those spines of yours?"

He pokes one. "Plenty sharp, laddie, but I dinnae think they'll kill this beast. I can try if you like, but you should get somewhere safe, my aim's not as good as it used to be."

I walk further into the dam, which is shaped in a slight semi-circle, so that I am around the corner from Malone and the zombie.

"Don't get too close, Malone," I say from my safe spot, tucking the spine Malone gave me into my fanny pack.

The answer I get is a sneeze and a shower of spines shooting into the wall opposite me.

"We're gonna have to clean that up before we leave," I whisper to myself. And then louder, to Malone, "Is it safe?"

"See for yourself," he yells back.

I turn the corner, and see the zombie, spines sticking out all over his head, not even slowing him down. He keeps chomping in our direction, as if willing himself close enough to actually get us in his mouth.

"Like I said, laddie, not enough to kill him," Malone says, running his paw over his back, which is visibly depleted of spines. "I'm guessing they don't go deep enough to kill the brain."

I agree, but maybe there's a solution to that problem. I unzip my fanny pack and dig through until I find what I'm looking for, a small shiny rock.

I can't believe I'm considering this, but a promise is a promise. And this is my only way to get to those raccoons. "Malone, I'm going to need you to distract him while I get close to this zombie's head."

"Are you daft?" the hedgehog demands, his eyes wide.

"If daft means what I think it means, then yes, probably," I answer, edging my way around the zombie, who strains against the wood holding him in place, as he tries to gain a few inches. "You keep him busy. I'm going to hammer in a few of your spines."

"You're mad as a hatter, laddie, but I'll give it a try," Malone replies, waddling over to the opposite side of the head. "You ready?"

Not at all, I think, but "Uh huh," is what comes out of my suddenly numb mouth.

"Hey ugly!" Malone yells. "Care for a bite of tasty hedgehog?"

The zombie reacts as expected, turning his face toward Malone and snapping his teeth at him, a groan rumbling out of his fetid mouth. I pick out a spine sticking out of the very top of the zombie head and count to three. Nothing happens. I try again. One. Two. Three! Nothing.

"Hey laddie!" Malone yells my way.

"We need another idea!" I yell back, shuddering as the zombie head turns my way. I can't do this. What a stupid plan!

"What other idea?" Malone yells back.

"I dunno, another one!" I say, desperate, the rock in my hand feeling heavier and heavier.

"Maybe we could ...," Malone starts to say, and then shrieks as the zombie head lunges within an inch of him.

I leap forward, throwing the rock and hitting the spine in the zombie's head as hard as I can. The zombie turns my way with alarming speed.

"Eep!" I screech, and trip backwards, scrambling away on all fours.

I sit there, my heart beating so fast and so hard I think it might pop right out of my chest.

"Laddie?" Malone calls from the zombie's other side.

"I'm fine," I call back, my voice as shaky as a teenage human's. "Let's try again."

Malone grumbles some curse words, but acquiesces, yelling at the zombie again.

Again, the dead face swings away from me, and I undo my fanny pack, dropping it to the dirt floor so the zombie can't grab it. I get to my hind paws, picking up the rock I dropped in my haste to not be eaten. I pick out another spine, this one at the back of the skull, and count to three twice before I get up the courage to strike it with all my force.

This time I'm ready for the reaction, and I spring away from the teeth that come at me, slamming into the wall of the dam and turning to run.

Only I'm not moving. Why aren't I moving? I dare to glance behind me and horror of horrors, the zombie has the end hairs of my tail clamped in his teeth!

"No," I whisper, straining away from death. I don't feel a thing. Is this what it's supposed to feel like? Death? The end? He's just got the hair of my tail, not the actual bone or muscle, but I can't rip free.

I clamp both paws around the branch closest to me, hearing Malone yell at the zombie, fear deepening his voice, but the dead man has me and he knows it. He pulls, and my hind paws leave claw marks in the dirt floor of the dam. The branch breaks off with a crack and in that split-second I know I'm done for. I turn towards the maw of teeth and yell all my terror at him. "I might be the last raccoon on Earth!" I shove the branch into the teeth ahead of me, wrapping my hind paws around it and pushing as hard as I can.

I hear another crack, and I force myself to open one eye. My tail is next to my face, quivering. I look down the branch I rode into this monster's mouth and follow its trajectory out the back of the zombie's skull.

"Ye did it, laddie!" squeals Malone, coming around the side and fairly bouncing on his toes. He pulls me by the shoulders, and I force my paws to release the branch, and wiggle backwards on the dirt floor until I am shaking next to the hedgehog.

"I did it," I whisper, the adrenaline receding to leave nausea and numbness. I fall forward onto my face and let the darkness take me for a while.

# CHAPTER TWELVE

"Trip," calls a voice that sounds a bit like my den mother. She doesn't smell like her though, that sweet combination of cardamom and scones. The owner of this voice smells like wet dog … and wood?

My eyes fly open wide. The dam. I'm in the dam and there's a beaver standing over me looking concerned.

"Steady on, laddie," Malone says, his hand on my shoulder as I struggle to sit up.

"Here, take a little drink of water," Mrs. King says, handing me a battered plastic cup filled with water. I take a sip and then another, my eyes flicking to the dead zombie still stuck head-first in the dam.

Malone follows my gaze and waves his paws dismissively. "He's dead this time, for sure. Mrs. King and I poked him with a stick."

"I never should have doubted you, Trip," Mrs. King says with a broad grin. Ha! Little does she know.

She takes back the cup, and I pick my fanny pack off the dirt floor, securing it around my waist with shaking paws. "So, we're square?"

Mrs. King points to a few logs she's dragged into the dam. "Just help me push these into place, and I will consider your debt repaid in full."

It takes a little practice, but Mrs. King is a patient teacher and we maneuver two logs over the zombie's head and two in front of him. The beaver gives her final instructions and then waddles out of the dam. When she gets into position on the outside of the dam's wall, she knocks, and we start to push the logs as she pulls the zombie out from the other side. River water starts to pour in, and I have to fight every instinct telling me to run, to get back to the surface. I imagine Pickles' determined face, and that gives me the courage to stay put, pushing and pushing at the logs until the zombie head slides out with a popping sound. As I keep the pressure on from the inside, Mrs. King said she will be slapping mud onto the outside of the structure, and Malone picks up his discarded spines from the floor all around me and starts hammering them into the wood at odd angles using my small rock, securing these new logs to the old logs of the dam. He's about halfway done when Mrs. King reappears on the inside, carrying piles of mud mixed with plant life. She begins pushing this mixture into the cracks between the logs. She goes back out to gather mud three more times before Malone runs out of spines to hammer.

The river water slows to a trickle and then finally stops entirely, and the dam is snug and waterproof like there never was a zombie head stuck in it. I'm wiped, Malone looks done in, and even the beaver has slowed down, rubbing at her non-existent neck.

Seriously, have you ever noticed how beavers seem to go from head to back with no real neck in between? The things you notice when you're tired.

Mrs. King leads the way back to the exit and Malone and I grab on to her tail without even being asked. I'm holding it together by sheer force of will at this point, too exhausted to worry about my underwater journey, and before I can start to panic about it, we've surfaced.

"Golden garburators, let's never do that again," I choke out, dropping to my knees to kiss the sandy beach.

Malone doesn't go that far, but trundles over to the burrow where we left Pal sleeping, sticking his head inside.

"My kits will be hungry," Mrs. King says, dropping onto all fours to stretch, her huge beaver tail pointed at the sky.

I sigh, taking the hint, no rest for the wicked or the wiped. I haul myself to all fours again, as Pal rolls out of his burrow, sleepy but following the hedgehog.

"All done?" he asks with a deep hoot.

"All snug again, thanks to these two," Mrs. King announces, slapping me on the back with enough force to knock me back to my knees.

We drag ourselves back to the camp, where we find Sonar curled up with the kits all around her. She opens one golden eye at our approach, and yawns, prodding the small beavers into alertness. Pal swoops low over the group to see everyone is safe and then takes off into the sky to catch up with the humans ahead of us. I mark his direction with my eyes and hope I don't lose his trail.

"Breakfast time, kits," Mrs. King announces as her children swarm her, bumping noses and heads. "Let's get these fine animals some fish before they continue their journey."

I ramble down to sit next to Ginger, who is licking himself clean of sand, a useless endeavor while we sit on a beach, but I'm smart enough not to point that out.

"So?" I ask.

He shakes his head. "I don't know, Trip, I think the dam will hold us if we try to walk across it. I tried it, and there are spots to avoid, but I'd rather risk it than try to swim. But my bigger worry is that Mrs. King is going to have a heck of a job keeping all those young beavers safe."

"We trained them as best we could," Sonar puts in, looking older than I've ever seen her look. "We tried to cram everything General Wally taught us into one night, but let's be honest. They're babies."

We throw a glance at the water where the "babies" are diving and harassing the river fish with an expertise none of us will ever show.

"We could bring them with us," Malone suggests, examining his half-bald tail with disapproving eyes.

"Maybe on the way back," I reply. I'm not sure what we'll find ahead of us at that camp. And I already feel like I have too much responsibility on my shoulders.

We fill up on tasty fresh fish courtesy of our aquatic rodent friends, and then head out into the forest. The kits line up to salute us and Sonar can't stop glancing over her shoulder at them, dragging her paws through the sand of the beach.

"You could stay behind with the beavers," Ginger says, seeing another opportunity to keep the young cat safe. "We will pick you up on the way back, and you could help Mrs. King keep them safe."

I think for a minute she's going to agree, but then she sets her jaw in that way that cats can and points her tail and her nose in the direction of the forest. "I will not give up my mission."

We stick close to the ground, our eyes and ears open for zombies, in a tight group. This side of the river must have been a camping type of park for humans, because we find small sealed garbage cans along the way. I know this is not true for every mammal, but garbage cans are reassuring to raccoons. It means easy access to food, and a place to store it until we can get it into our stomachs. I pat my fanny pack as I climb up and onto one of the garbage cans to root through it.

"Carrots, old cheese, ooh, a half-finished bag of chips," I list off, passing the first two items down to Ginger, who wrinkles his nose in response, and passes them back to Malone. The hedgehog takes a big bite of the carrot. Sonar is hungry enough to try the cheese, but she turns a little green at the taste. Actually, the cheese was a little green to begin with so maybe that reaction is normal. Cats are so picky.

We walk another twenty minutes, and now I'm scanning the skies for a sign of Pal, hoping he can reassure me that we're still going the right way. I catch sight of another garbage can attached to a tree trunk and scramble up that tree next. I'm actually starting to feel useful for the first time in ages. No one can find treasure out of garbage like a raccoon can.

"Ew. Old diapers," I say, picking my way past the worst of it. "Oh, I think I smell ... something nutty ... maybe a granola bar?"

"How can you smell anything in that?" Malone calls up from the forest floor. From the sound of his voice, I can tell he's holding his tiny nose.

"Anything that might have been alive at some point?" Ginger calls up to me, hope in his voice.

I tuck a half-eaten granola bar into my fanny pack and keep digging, until only my tail would be visible out of the top of the garbage can. Down further I go, until my hands scrape the metal of the bottom, where at last I find the mother lode — a half-eaten chicken carcass.

"Thank you, Gods of the Garbage Dump," I whisper, sniffing at it for a rancid stench and finding none. I speak louder now, so they can hear me outside the can. "Ginger, you are going to be *so* happy."

That's when the garbage lid slams closed above me, narrowly missing my tail.

"What the ...?" I squawk, scrambling back up towards the lid, through the diapers and food I had dismissed as too rotten. I reach the top and press up with both paws, but the lid won't move. I push with my head and my paws, calling for Ginger. I hear hissing from outside the can, and then the can I'm trapped in is moving, and I hear Malone cursing a blue streak.

"Let him go!" Malone yells, and then sneezes.

I don't hear any dramatic screams of pain, and a second later I hear Malone cursing his lack of spines.

The sound of a cat flying through the air signals Ginger's attack, like a loud wind with a caterwaul thump, but it seems to have no effect on my situation. Would a zombie pick up a garbage can? I flip over ungracefully and kick with my hind paws against the lid, screeching at the top of my lungs.

"Trip!" Sonar calls, her voice tiny and receding. I'm being taken away from my friends! Panic takes over and I scramble all over the can, scratching at the bag in the can until my claws find metal. I yell. I curse. I call for my friends. But I can't hear them anymore. I can't hear anything anymore. I'm in the dark and alone and I sink into a stupor surrounded by the garbage I love.

# CHAPTER THIRTEEN

I don't know how much time has passed. I lie on my bed of garbage, rocking back and forth as I am carried away to my fate. Below me is the comforting stench of rotting things. Above me is a metal lid that I can't wrestle open. I tell myself to rest up so I can fight my way free even as I feel that lingering voice in my mind that says I'm done for. I'm no fighter. I'm a negotiator. A trader. A hugger of stronger animals who protect me.

I'm jerked out of my zoned-out state when the can I'm locked in takes an upward swing and then comes to a complete stop with a bang.

"Cho!" I hear a female human voice yell.

I press myself up against the lid again, carefully, and it opens slightly, enough for me to see that I'm inside a human building.

"Where the heck is that guy?"

Whoever Cho is, he's not answering, and I watch a

large woman walk away from my position and out of my sight. I hear a door slam and I push up on the lid again. It's still locked shut, but I can get it up high enough to see that I'm on top of a table in a narrow hallway filled with shelves. I'm pretty close to the edge of the table, so I decide to do what I'm best at — trip. I slam myself back and forth inside the garbage can, edging myself towards the end of the table until I'm tumbling towards the floor. Shaking the banging noise from my ears, I struggle out of the garbage and I'm free! I'm racing to the opposite door the woman went through, hurling myself into the darkness beyond. I press myself against the wall of this new room, trying to catch my breath as my eyes adjust to the dark room.

"Who's that, mommy?"

I hear the question and stop breathing entirely, because it came from a tiny baby raccoon in a cage above my head.

"Great golden garburators," I whisper, turning around in a circle to see cages stacked on cages of raccoons. Big ones, small ones, black ones, brown ones, gray ones … it's more raccoons than I've ever seen in my life.

Before I can do any more than stare, dumbstruck, I hear human voices from the hallway. I switch to panic mode again, streaking through the room haphazardly, looking for a hiding place.

"Here!" calls a voice in a corner, and I dart that way,

totally running on instinct. The young raccoon who called me points behind her cage, so I skid to a stop, somehow squeezing myself in between the outside of the cage and the wall it's stacked up against. There's no way I'm going to fit until she shoves an upside-down bottle of water out of the way from the inside of her cage. Now I'm tucked in behind it, looking at the two humans who have entered the room through the distortion of water.

"It can't have gone far!" the woman who carried me away from my friends declares.

"Are you sure it was a raccoon?" asks the other human, peering into the corners of the room.

"I didn't have a lot of time to check," the woman says, her voice defensive. "I saw the striped tail sticking out of the top of the garbage and slammed it shut and then suddenly, I swear, I was attacked by two rabid cats and a hedgehog."

The other human stops searching, and the raccoon who moved the water bottle squints at me with a very curious look. "A what?" asks the human, incredulously.

"I know how crazy that sounds," the woman replies. "But you said you were looking for fresh test subjects, so I grabbed the garbage and ran."

"Test subjects?" I repeat in a low voice, casting my eyes around the room again at all the cages.

"I'm going to check the hallway again," the woman

announces. "Maybe it escaped into the dorms."

The humans leave, noisily closing the door behind them, and two hundred pairs of masked eyes swing my way.

"Oh boy," I breathe, slowly twisting myself back out from behind the cage and turning to speak to the raccoon who saved me. "Thank you."

She smiles at me, pressing a paw to her chest. "My name is Sumi. Who are you? What are you doing here?"

"I'm ... Trip," I say, coming out from my hiding place. "And I don't know what I'm doing here, really. I was in the forest and they grabbed me out of a garbage can."

Many voices start talking at once.

"Where are you from?"

A whistle from Sumi stops the barrage of questions. "Hey! Give the raccoon a minute. He just got here, and he's on the run."

"Well, he'd better keep running," says an older raccoon from right beside Sumi's cage. "If he doesn't want to end up in one of these cages with us."

Now all the masked faces are nodding in unison.

"The door over there leads out to the forest," the old raccoon says. His fur is mostly gray, but his belly has been shaved, revealing a pink skin I can't help but stare at. He notices and drops from his upright stance back onto all fours and turns away from me.

"Don't mind Winter," Sumi says, pulling my attention back to her. "He's right. You should position yourself next to that door and wait for a human to come through. We'll distract them so you can bolt out."

She smiles kindly at me, and I look around at all the other cages to find similar encouraging looks on masked faces.

"But what about you?" I ask, trying to count the number of raccoons in this room and failing. "I was looking for a camp with raccoons, and I think I've found it."

The raccoon named Winter snorts. "You were looking for this camp? Are you an idiot?"

"Winter," Sumi calls out, but the old mammal whips back around to face me. I try really hard not to take a step back from his cold eyes.

"Don't you know what this camp is?" he hisses through the bars at me.

In the cage above him, I see a mother raccoon put her paws protectively over her daughter's ears.

"This is a death camp, buddy," Winter says. "This is where raccoons come to die."

There's a ringing in my ears, so it takes me a few minutes to notice that Sumi is calling my name.

"Trip? Are you okay?" she asks.

I can't believe she's asking me if I'm okay while she's stuck inside a cage at a camp where raccoons are on the endangered list. She might be asking because I just ran into the corner and threw up my fishy lunch. Raccoons hate throwing up almost as much as we hate locked compost bins. Both are a huge waste of food.

I climb up and onto the counter and run the taps, scooping water into my mouth and rinsing it clean, feeling guilty that I am free to do that.

"What's it like out there?" asks a voice from a cage next to me.

"How long have you been in here?" I ask the raccoon, who's about my age, but a lot skinnier. His arms are pink and shaved, and his mask is a soft gray. He smells like rainy mornings and carrot cake.

"Don't know," he admits, scratching at his shaved arm. "Are the zombies still out there?"

I shudder, and that must be enough of an answer, because he drops his paws from the bars.

"Where is your gaze?" asks a tiny voice in another cage above me. I rise up on my hind legs so that I can meet her eyes. She's an adorable little raccoon with freckles that remind me of Pickles. She smells like blue cotton candy.

"I don't know," I answer honestly; I don't see them here. "My name is Trip, what's yours?"

"Sheela," she replies with a smile. "And this is my brother Nick."

Nick is even smaller, and I can't see their mother in

the cage with them, but I don't want to upset them by asking if they're alone. My heart is getting heavier with every raccoon I meet.

"Is that a purse?" she asks, pointing to my fanny pack.

"Kind of," I say with a smile, digging into it for the half granola bar I know is in there and handing it to her and Nick.

We hear sounds from outside the door, and I drop into the sink, out of view. I peek up in time to see the exit door open and get a glimpse of the forest outside before Duke follows another human into the room.

"Cho, I need to see Innes now," Duke says, rubbing at his bald head, not even looking around at the raccoons staring at him. "I don't know what she was thinking ..."

"You know the rules, Duke," Cho says, opening the door to the hallway I had fled, and pushing him in. "You have to ..."

Their voices recede and I slowly raise my head up in wonder. Duke's here? My eyes are fixed to that exit door, expecting to see Uma and Sarah right behind him.

"Trip," Sumi calls, and I scramble out of the sink and back down to floor level in a clumsy tumble of arms and legs.

"You have to go," she says, pointing at the door I'm already staring at. "The next time that door opens, you have to be ready to run out. The raccoon nearest that door, his name is Beast. He'll help."

I nod, still totally distracted, waiting to see Sarah. I know, as soon as she sees me and sees this room full of raccoons, she'll know what to do. I take a step away from Sumi, and then realize, I have to know.

"What did Winter mean?" I ask, looking over at his cage. He's facing the wall, so I don't think he's going to answer, so I whisper this at Sumi: "When he ... Winter ... said this is a camp where raccoons come to ... die?"

She glances around, and waves me a bit closer, so that the little raccoons won't hear. "The humans capture us and do tests. All kinds of tests. I don't know if they mean to kill us. Or if they are bad mammals. But either way ..."

"But raccoons die?" I ask, inhaling her scent for the first time — a mix of apples and cookie dough.

"Raccoons have died," she answers slowly, shifting her dark eyes away from me. Close up, I can see that her hind paw has been shaved too. "But they keep finding new raccoons and bringing them in here. We thought that's what you were brought here for, but you came looking for us?"

"It wasn't exactly how I planned to get in here, but yes," I say. "There are no raccoons at my camp."

Her eyes go wide, so I raise my paws, trying to reassure her. "There never were. My humans, they aren't experimenting on us at all. They are good mammals."

She cocks her head curiously. "Your humans?"

"Yes, we live with the humans," I explain, cognizant that the entire room is listening to us again. I dig into my fanny pack again and pass her my last few berries.

"But you said there were no raccoons at your camp."

"Erm ... yes."

"Then who is 'we'?" she asks, stuffing berries into her mouth.

The door slams again, and I flatten against her cage, watching Cho walk back across the room.

"Go, now!" Sumi hisses, and I skitter across the room, dodging under shelves stacked high with cages, listening to my raccoon brethren encourage me. I don't know why they're helping me, a coward, escape, when they are all trapped, but I can't think about it now.

"Stop!" whispers a voice above me and I flatten on the ground under a cage. Cho's feet have stopped.

"Go left!" says a different voice, and I follow their orders, because they can see what I cannot. Also, because it's nice to not have to make decisions for a little while. I duck, dive, and scramble my way to the door until I'm behind the cage right next to the door that leads to the forest. The raccoon in this cage is twice my size, and well-named. Beast looks at me, gives me a wink of encouragement, and as soon as Cho opens the door, throws himself into a frenzy of howls and whistles.

"What the heck?" Cho says, turning to look around

as the whole room erupts into a cacophony of screeches, growls and yips.

I throw myself out the door and clamber around the corner, stopping to catch my breath. Now that I'm outside, I can see this compound is very like our own, with distinct buildings, and a wooden fence all around the perimeter and a forest mere steps away.

Cho finally exits the raccoon cage room. "Stupid raccoons," he says as he throws a bag over his shoulder.

I watch him walk to the swinging gate built into the fence, where an odd-looking orange dog stands on guard. I say odd-looking because it's got no tail at all, just a little stump, but when Cho gets close, she leaps to her feet and her entire back end starts shaking like she's happy to see him. She reminds me a little of Emmy when she walks, but she looks like a chubby fox, minus the tail of course. Cho ignores her, actually shoves her out of the way as he opens the door and I stare as he walks into the forest. That's my way out. I need to run. I need to find Ginger and Pal. I'm pulling on my whiskers so hard that my face hurts.

The odd dog is still facing the gate, her back end slowing down in its excitement when two other dogs on long chains approach. I press myself further into this wall, hoping they can't smell me, because these dogs don't look odd. They look dangerous.

"If it isn't the guard princess," the larger one sneers. And by larger one, I mean the one that could eat Emmy in a single bite. He's got shoulders like a water buffalo, I swear. Okay, I've never seen a water buffalo, but I imagine they look like this dog.

The orange dog whips around her sausage-shaped body to face them. "What do you want, Moose?" she demands, surprising all of us a bit with her boldness.

"What do you want, Moose?" the other big dog mimics in a high-pitched voice, causing Moose to laugh uproariously. "What a kitten."

Odd dog doesn't like that one bit, and bares her teeth at her two opponents.

"Let's go, Zach, before the little princess drops her crown," Moose says, turning tail and sauntering back in the direction he had come.

She watches them go, almond-shaped eyes narrowed, and then returns to her vigilance, watching the gate. I wonder if she will chase me into the forest. Probably. She's not on a chain at all, but she seems nervous and high-strung. And she reminds me of Wally and Sonar in her attention to duty. Something raccoons don't think about at all by the way. That makes me glance back at the raccoons I just left behind. I'll need help to get them out of here. I can't do it on my own.

"I've gotta find Ginger," I repeat to myself, backing

up along the wall slowly. Or if I can find Pal I can send a message to …

"Who's Ginger?"

"Gah!" I screech, whipping around in fright to find the odd dog from the gate, sitting on her haunches. She looks at my paws in their karate-chop position and tilts her head in question.

"I … You …," I point to her, and then back at the gate. "How?"

"I'm quicker than I look," she explains, licking her lips. "Who's Ginger?"

"My … my friend," I say, slowly backing away from the dog. Dogs traditionally chase and torment raccoons where I come from. At least they did before the zombies appeared.

She steps forward and sits down again. "Oh, another raccoon? Have you checked the room behind you? Loads of raccoons in there."

"I … no, he's not a raccoon," I say, glancing behind me and taking another step back.

She matches my movements and sits for a third time. "Not a raccoon? Too bad. We love raccoons here. He could make lots of new friends."

I snort before I can stop myself, but instead of attacking me for my insolence, this weird dog just tilts her head at me again. I have no idea what this canine is up to.

"You know they're not here by choice, right?" I ask, putting all my snacks on the table. "Your humans, they grab raccoons from the forest and bring them here and then experiment on them."

This time it's she who snorts, and even her snort is cute. "Don't be crazy. Experiment on raccoons? Ridiculous. They saved the raccoons. Like they saved me."

"They saved you?" I ask, remembering how Cho treated her as he went through the fence.

"Well, sort of," she replies, a little self-consciously. "I was lost and I saw this convoy of humans and animals, and I sort of ... tagged along."

"Uh huh," I say, understanding more than she could ever know. It's a lot like I felt joining Pickles' fellowship. The odd mammal out. But this dog is no coward. She's useful.

"But they let me stay," she says, a little defensively, perhaps sensing how much I understood. "Kept me safe from the dead ones out there."

We both look out over the fence at a few of the zombies wandering the outskirts of the camp and share a shudder.

"Hey! Princess!" yells a deep voice from somewhere behind me. I freeze in place as the odd dog dashes around me to stand so that her back is pressed against mine. I look at the fence in front of me. Could I climb over it? What about the zombies on the other side?

"Don't move," she hisses at me, and then in a louder voice to the other dogs, "Don't come over here! I'm ... um ... taking care of some personal business!"

Snickers from the male dogs and then, "When you're finished with your make-up, your highness, you might want to take a look at your little castle. We left you some ... presents."

More snickers, and I feel the odd dog's tension through her tail-less body. I can't move from fright, and it's a good thing. I think she was blocking me from the other dogs' sight with her own body.

"Jerks. My name's Diana. What's yours?" she asks, her back still pressed against mine.

"Um, Trip," I manage to gasp out.

"Welcome, Trip. Are you hungry?" she asks, and then bounds off towards the edge of the fence. I'm so surprised that I follow on wobbly legs, glad the sun is going down and that I might be able to escape under cover of darkness.

"Stand guard," she says, digging with all four paws, snuffling in the dirt.

"You're joking, right?" I say, wondering if dogs keep their common sense in their tails, and whether this dog is lacking her tail and therefore nuts.

"Did a zombie bite off your tail?" I ask, hoping for her sake it's not attached to someone's hat.

She grimaces. "No, a human. A live human. It's a thing

they do to corgi pups. Don't ask me why. They think it makes us look cute. I think I'd rather have my tail than look cute."

I silently agree as she pulls a half-eaten pork chop out of her hole in the ground and I forget every mean thing I ever thought about dogs. Even the ones who would take turns guarding a trash bin so that I was trapped inside for days on end, slowly eating my way down the bin, hoping one of my siblings would notice I was missing and come looking. Sharing a meal with a non-raccoon is something I had never done before Pickles and Ginger came into my life. We shared a bag of cat food in a convenience store many moons ago. Diana and I share the pork chop, passing it back and forth like we grew up in the same burrow. She smacks her lips just like I do, and has the same sense of hygiene, washing her paws in a low water barrel beside us. This is the most relaxed I've seen her look and it's weird that she feels that way around a raccoon. I decide corgis are not normal dogs. They're better.

"So, Ginger?" she prompts again.

"A cat," I reply. She doesn't have the traditional canine reaction to raccoons, maybe she's cool with felines as well. "He's my best friend. We got separated when one of your humans raccoon-napped me."

"Not that again," she says, licking at the bone before dropping it back in the hole and covering it back up with dirt. "I'm sure they meant to help you."

"Have you ever been in that room? With the raccoons?" I ask, washing my hands in the same low rain barrel she used before.

"No."

"I have," I say. "And I'm telling you, those raccoons were not rescued. They want to leave. They helped me escape."

Diana looks worried now, and I decide this is a good time for me to leave. "I appreciate your help, but I have to go before Cho comes back and locks me in a cage too."

I point at the gate. "I can go out that way, right?"

"I guess, yes, you can," she answers, but looks sad at the prospect. "Are you sure you need to go? Maybe the raccoons you spoke to are confused. I could explain it to them. And then you could stay."

I shake my head. "Sorry to burst your bubble, my canine friend, but you've got it wrong. If my humans were here …"

"Your humans?" she asks, rising to her feet again, her backside wiggling anew in excitement. "You have other live humans? Are they your pets?"

"Yeah, Uma and Sarah. I keep expecting to see them but …," my voice trails off because Diana's back end has stopped. In fact, if she had a tail, I'm pretty sure it would be between her legs right now. "Diana? What's wrong?"

"Uma and Sarah?" she whispers, her bottom lip shaking slightly.

"Yeah … why?" I start to reply, but she suddenly growls sharply and her shoulders go up.

"What?" I say, backing up from the suddenly hostile mammal in front of me. "Diana, what's wrong?"

"Your humans are the enemy," she growls from between pointy teeth I had not noticed till this moment. I've backed up all the way to the fence now, and I can feel the wood behind me, poking me and beckoning me at the same time.

"Enemy? What are you talking about?" I say, running my paws over the wood behind my back and finding a knothole. I wrap one paw around it and point at a spot behind Diana with my other paw. "What is THAT?!"

Diana whips around to face the new foe just as I expected her to, and I scramble up the wooden fence, getting up about halfway before I run out of knotholes to stick my feet in, and look back down at the dog who I thought was my friend. She barks at me, but not in a scary way. I can tell she's conflicted.

"Diana, my humans aren't enemies," I call down, my heart sad at this turn of events. "And I'm sure as heck not your enemy."

"I am a loyal dog," she says through her teeth, tears falling from her eyes.

"Of course you are," I say, well aware of what loyalty

means to the canine species. Emmy's two best friends were the most loyal animals on the planet, shielding her from their pets when they turned into zombies and giving up their lives to save her.

"I am a loyal dog," she whispers again, walking away from me, no wiggle in her step at all.

"Enemies," I repeat, shaking my head as well, and then suddenly, I realize what this means. If Diana knows their names ... and thinks they're her enemies. "Then Sarah and Uma are here," I whisper to the night sky. I'm still looking up when Pal flies into my sight and I grin. Thank the Gods of the Garbage. My friends are here.

# CHAPTER FOURTEEN

P al helps me climb to the top of the fence, and we
embrace like we haven't seen each other in years.

"We thought you were dead," he hoots into my ear.

"You always think I'm dead," I reply, squeezing my
friend tighter. "Where is everybody else?"

He pulls away, leaving behind little feathers all over
my fur, and looks around at the camp curiously. "About
a half-day behind me, I think. Ginger is pushing everyone
like some kind of herding animal."

I point out the building holding the raccoons. "I found
them, Pal. The raccoons. Every raccoon in the area is
trapped in that building."

Quickly, I run through everything that has happened
to me since being raccoon-napped in a garbage can. Pal
hops off the fence suddenly, flying low over the grass
behind us, scoops something and swoops back up to the

fence. In his mouth are crickets, and we munch on them as I tell the rest of my story.

"You saw Duke?" Pal asks. "We gave up following them when you were taken and followed your trail instead."

"He walked through that building," I say with a nod, "and I think Sarah and Uma are here too."

That's when Diana walks by on her patrol, glances up at the fence, and does a double-take when she sees us.

"Diana," I call down from the safety of the top of the fence, "this is my friend Pallas. Pallas, that's Diana. She's a corgi."

Both of them look at me like I'm crazy to be talking to a dog, but I've got an idea, and ideas make me less scared than usual. They always have.

"Um, hey Diana," Pal hoots after a minute. "Nice to meet you."

Diana looks like she wants to say hi, but can't quite do it, so I ask, "Hey, what presents did Moose and Zach leave for you in your castle?"

"Castle?" Pal hoots in question.

"It's not really …," Diana says before she can stop herself. "It's just my pup tent. They call it a castle."

"Oh, because it's fancy?" Pal asks.

Diana drops her gaze, finding the dirt under her paws suddenly super interesting. "No. Not fancy."

"They're bullies," I explain to Pal, following my

instincts. "They call Diana a princess and call her pup tent a castle."

She raises her long snout my way in surprise. She doesn't know I've been bullied my whole life. Raccoons are the most bullied animals in a city. We get bullied by cats, dogs, humans, squirrels, sparrows, chipmunks ... You name the mammal, and I guarantee I have been cursed out by it. It might be because we treat food as communal, or it might be the masked faces that make us look like little thieves, or maybe it's the fact that we don't really respect personal boundaries and love to hug it out, but I know how to recognize a bully. And Moose and Zach are prime examples.

"Oh," Pal says, looking back and forth between us, his head pivoting and rotating unnaturally. "So the presents they left for Diana were ..."

"Poop," Diana says with a humiliated sob. "They left behind poop."

"Hold my cricket," I say, handing the headless insect to Pal. I climb back down the wall of the fence towards Diana.

"What are you doing?" Diana snuffles at me.

Instead of answering, I wrap my arms around her. She stiffens up immediately, but I just squeeze harder. I've brought a raging hamster a long way with my hugs, I know how therapeutic they can be. Diana slowly relaxes, turning her snout into my neck and snuffling tears into my fur.

"Ahem, mammals?" Pal asks. "I hate to interrupt, but I need to fly back and find the rest of our friends."

Diana stiffens up again. "You're bringing your friends here?"

"Yes," I say, still very close to the dog and hoping she doesn't turn hostile again. "But first, I need you to tell me where Sarah and Uma are."

She immediately shakes her head. "I can't betray my humans. I won't help you invade our camp."

"Invade?" Pal snorts, and promptly pulls a classic Trip maneuver, falling off the fence. He can fly though, so he catches himself a foot from the ground and flaps over to us. "That's the opposite of what we want."

Diana's head swings back and forth between us. "But …"

"Diana, I came here for those raccoons," I say, pointing at the building again, "and Sarah and Uma came here with one of your humans, Duke, to set up some kind of trading opportunities or something."

I look at Pal for more clarity, but the truth is, neither of us is sure what Sarah and Uma wanted. Or what happened to them when they got here.

"No," Diana says. "That can't be right."

"I'm just telling you what we heard," I say. "They said they were coming with Duke to trade for something."

"But how did you know we had raccoons here?" Diana asks.

I hesitate, but Pal pokes me in the back, so I say, "Duke was wearing a raccoon-skin hat, and our friend Wally overheard that there were lots of raccoons being kept here at Duke's camp."

Diana shudders dramatically, her shake starting up at her head and flowing all the way down to her wiggly back end. "I hated that hat. So creepy to wear some other mammal's tail on your head."

Seeing as this particular dog didn't have a tail, I guessed that held a special significance.

"Can you help us find Sarah and Uma?" I ask again, taking Diana's face in my paws. "Please? We need their help to free the raccoons."

"This is crazy, I just got out of there," I say, my teeth chattering slightly at what we're about to do. Dogs, it turns out, are even wackier than hamsters. And as brave as cats. Why do I keep making friends with crazy fearless animals?

"I told you, I'm not helping you do anything until I hear from these raccoons directly. I think they're happy to be here," Diana says, watching the door to the building I just escaped. "Plus, you said Pal needs time to find the rest of your friends and get back here."

"But what about Sarah and Uma?" I ask.

"Nothing will happen to them tonight," she assures me. "Everyone's down for the night. Trust me. I know the operations of this camp like the back of my paw."

"You want me to trust you, but you don't trust me," I grumble.

She hangs her head before answering. "I know, but I've had some bad experiences with other mammals in the past. I only trust what I can smell, hear, and see. In that order."

"What happened?" I ask, delaying us and this nutty mission as long as I can. Maybe Ginger is closer than Pal thinks he is. Maybe we don't have to go back in there alone. Maybe sense will rain down from the heavens like Timbits and this dog will knock off this crazy mission.

Great. Now I'm hungry again.

She hesitates, so I wait. I know how hard it can be to admit you've been the object of abuse. I used to joke about it as a way to cover up my pain. The truth is, Diana is totally changing my view on dogs. I mean, Emmy used to talk about her dog partners saving her from the zombies, but I thought they were just oddities. Maybe there were more dogs like Diana. And maybe dogs had the same problems as the rest of us.

"I don't know if I told you, but before all of this, I had a gaze," I say, the words coming out of my mouth before I can stop them. "They were my family. My community.

So, of course I miss them. But the truth is they were always making fun of me. Pushing me around. Stealing my stuff. Making fun of my friendships with the chipmunks next door."

Diana doesn't say anything, but I recognize the look of pity in her eyes, so I keep talking, "But now, back at my camp, I have this pack of friends — Ginger and Sonar are two cats you will meet, and you've already met Pallas, but Wally, Hannah, and Pickles are three other cats I live with, and there's also a hamster named Emmy."

She laughs, a lovely sound. "That's a whole lot of cats."

I nod, smiling for the first time in a while, feeling the fear recede a little bit as I remember their faces. "I'm still not sure I belong amongst them, to be honest."

Diana drops her eyes from mine, but I keep talking. "They're brave and loyal and so smart, and not at all clumsy or cowardly," I say, admitting it, and feeling the shame rise. "I try very hard to fit in, but the truth is, I don't know that I do, and that's probably because of how I grew up, being bullied and ridiculed. It has nothing to do with today or my life after the apocalypse. I just know that those cats and that hamster and that owl make me feel like I should be a better mammal. They make want to be brave and smart. So, I try. For them. You know what I mean?"

She nods, but doesn't speak, and I guess this isn't the time to talk about whatever she's been through.

"I've never told anyone that," I say as I reach up and grab the door handle. "You ready?"

"My pet used to put me in these shows," she says quietly.

I let go of the door handle and turn to listen respectfully.

"They were dog shows, and there were lots of different kinds of dogs competing," she says, looking at the ground. "I used to win prizes. I used to win every year."

She stops talking and I say, "That sounds good though, isn't it Diana? Your pet must have been happy with you."

She shakes her head and takes a few gulping breaths before continuing. "I lost. Last year. I lost. I don't know why, I don't know what I did wrong. I just lost."

I pet her back, because her sadness is coming off her in waves, and I feel tears welling up in my own eyes in response.

"I'm sure it wasn't anything you did," I say.

She shudders. "My pet left me at the show. Just left me there. Like I was an old bone. Alone. Leashed to a chair."

"Gods of the Garbage," I say, sadder than I've been since finding those raccoons caged in that room. "That's terrible, Diana. I'm so sorry."

"She said she loved me," Diana hiccups, fighting back tears. "She told me all the time. But I shouldn't have believed her. She never showed it. She lied. No one who loves you leaves you tied to a chair because you don't win a stupid ribbon."

"No, they don't," I agree, wishing I could take her pain away.

"I only believe what I smell, hear, and see," she says, meeting my eyes. "You see? You can't believe what you feel. That's not real."

I hesitate, because seeing a dog as a friend is very new, but mustering up all of my courage, I take her beautiful fox-face in my paws and say, "Then believe this: I smell like your friend, so don't forget my scent. I sound like your ally, so memorize my voice. And I look like … well, I don't know what I look like, probably a deranged masked clown at this point, but I will not leave you. Not while I'm alive."

"Really?" she asks.

"Really," I reply, and I mean it. "I mean, look at all the trouble I'm going to just so you can confirm what I already know to be true about the raccoons at this camp. Would I bother with that if I was just using you?"

"No," she sniffs.

"Any chance that was enough to convince you not to go in there?"

"No," she sniffs.

"Didn't think so," I sigh, turning back to the door. "Ready?"

"Ready," she says.

I open the door, and she sticks her snout in, holding it open so we can both shuffle in. It's pitch dark inside, but in the seconds it takes for our eyes to adjust, Beast recognizes me.

"What in the name of compost are you doing back in here?" he hisses at me.

"Not my idea," I hiss back, trying to direct Diana through the cages. The raccoons are whispering and rustling as we pass, and Diana is wide-eyed and quiet.

"Sumi," I call. "Sumi, I need you to talk to this dog for me."

"Sumi's not here," Winter says with a growl, eyeing my canine partner. "And I don't talk to dogs."

"Why not?" asks Diana.

Instead of answering, Winter points to his thigh, where a bite mark is still visible. A huge bite mark that could belong to a moose of a dog. Or a water buffalo.

"Oh," Diana says in a small voice.

"Where is Sumi?" I ask, scared that she's not here.

About a hundred paws answer my question, all pointing at the hallway where I started this offshoot adventure.

"She's getting tested," Winter says, a hint of sympathy in his usually gravelly voice.

"What does that mean?" Diana asks me, and then when I don't answer, she pulls on my tail. "Trip? What does that mean?"

"Stay here," I say, scampering to the hallway door. I look up at the cage that is eye-level with the window in the door. "I'm going in there. Can you see any humans?"

"What?"

"Just tell me if you see humans," I say, gritting my teeth so they don't chatter.

"No, but they could come back any minute," the voice from the cage says.

"Then we don't have much time," Diana says, scaring me into bumping my head on the door. "Oops, sorry!"

"You're like a ninja," I reply, rubbing at the top of my head before I reach for the doorknob.

I open it slowly, and we shuffle into the hallway, but Sumi's not here either.

"Do you know where this leads?" I ask Diana, pointing at the end of the hallway.

"No," she replies, sniffing at the next door. "But it smells terrible."

I open this door as well, this time without the benefit of a pair of raccoon eyes checking for humans. This room is full of horrible chemical smells and dimly lit like a horror show on TV. Two human legs can be seen at the far end of the room standing over a large metal table, and I cower in fright. Fortunately, the room is also covered in equipment and rolling furniture, so we dart from hiding spot to hiding spot. I slide under a low table, and beckon Diana over, but she's transfixed by something on that metal table.

"No reaction," a human male says. "Again."

I hear a growl from the same location, and then some coughing.

"Diana," I hiss at the dog, who is slowly approaching the human legs and now I'm pulling on my whiskers.

"I want another test," the other human says, and then she turns and sees Diana. "What is that dog doing in here?"

Both humans are now looking down at Diana, whose eyes are as big as I've ever seen them.

"Diana, what are you doing in here?" the male human asks, coaxing her backwards. Diana is resolute though, she dodges around him, and climbs a chair so that her front paws are on the metal table. I hear whispers from the table that I think I recognize.

"Hey!" the male voice exclaims, grabbing the dog around the waist.

Diana growls and twists, trying to get away, but she can't fight off two humans. "Trip! You were right! Get out! Get all of them out!"

And then they're gone. All three of them, through the door that leads to the hallway. I can hear Diana howling and barking, so I skitter out into the middle of the room. They won't hurt her, will they? She's their dog. What do I do?

"Trip?" says Sumi's voice.

I whip around. That voice came from the metal table. I clamber up the chair Diana used and onto the metal table where my friend lies. I can't catch my breath. I'm horrified. Sumi is chained to the table, her fur matted with blood, a huge bite mark on her back.

"Oh, Sumi," I whisper, putting my paws on her and then springing away. She's as hot as a lit barbeque.

"Trip," she whispers through a painful smile. "You came back."

"I did," I choke out, putting my paws on her hot face, caressing her mask. "I ran because I was scared, but I couldn't leave."

"You see what they do to us?" she asks, trying to look at her back and wincing at the effort. "They put us out to be bitten by a zombie, chained to a tree, and then they bring us back here to test their antidote."

I nod through my tears, the scent of apples and cookie dough starting to fade away. "I do. I understand."

"Those raccoons in that room," she says, eyelids fluttering. "They are your gaze now. Get them out, Trip. Save our gaze."

# CHAPTER FIFTEEN

I sit over Sumi's still body for far too long, stroking her fur, apologizing over and over again for my cowardice. I might have sat there until I, too, was captured for experimentation if not for the skylight above us that slowly fills the room with the sunrise. It's the buffet of colors that ripple over Sumi's fur that give me the strength to let her go. I butt heads with her the way my cats have taught me and look up at the skylight.

There's a cord hanging down from the skylight, and I use it to climb up and out of that horrible room. I don't look back down because my friend is gone, and she tasked me with a mission. To be honest, I feel a little numb. Like that time I got stuck in a restaurant cold room overnight. From the slightly sloped roof I can see the entire camp, but no one is stirring. It's too early. I walk towards the sunrise and see that I can climb to the next roof, which is flat. I walk across it as well, feeling the warmth of the sun trying to coax me back to life.

There's a skylight on this building as well, so I walk over and look down into the room below to see Sarah and Uma tied to a pole. I feel a spark of hope shove its way into the numbness around my heart. I pull at the sunroof from all angles, but this one is closed tight, so I walk to the edge of the roof and look down, unsurprised to see a pup tent below me, and Diana lying outside it attached by a collar around her neck to a long chain. She's the opposite of relaxed, her paws moving continuously, her ears flicking back and forth.

"Diana," I call, surprising myself with the deepness of my own voice. I clear my throat of sadness, wishing it were that easy to clear my heart, and call again. "Diana."

Diana hears me and leaps to her feet. "Trip! Oh, Trip, I'm so sorry I didn't believe you," Diana says, standing directly beneath me. "I saw ... I smelled ... your friend ..."

"Where are the bigger dogs?" I ask.

"On patrol," she answers. "Why?

Instead of answering, I climb down the side of the building falling the last two feet to land on my rump. I turn to look at the door — there's a combination lock on it. Wonderful.

"Trip, I want to help," Diana says.

"You've helped enough," I say, not turning around.

I know it's not fair to blame Diana, but this pain has to go somewhere. While Diana and I were exchanging sad stories, Sumi was ... I can't finish that thought. I pull at the lock, but it's no good. It's locked tight.

"Trip, I didn't know they were experimenting on your friends," she says. "I thought that's just where the raccoons lived. In that building."

"And Duke's raccoon tail hat?" I ask, glaring back at her. "How could you believe that a human like that could be 'saving' raccoons? Just leave me alone, Diana. I know where your loyalties lie."

I dismiss the distraught dog and look around on the ground for something I can use to break the lock. The rock in my fanny pack isn't big enough, but if I could find a big one —

"It's 1, 22, 43," Diana says, her voice so hoarse with tears I can barely understand her.

"Huh?"

"The combination," she repeats. "1, 22, 43."

My mouth drops open because I'd never considered that she knew how to open the lock, but I shake off my shock, and I turn the lock according to her instructions. Maybe I wasn't wrong about this dog.

"No, once around, and then the 1, and then back the other way to 22," she coaches me. "And then forward again all the way to 43."

There's a click and the lock drops open. I take it off

and open the door, peering inside. Sitting on the floor, with their hands tied behind their backs in the same position I saw through the skylight, sit Sarah and Uma.

"What in the world?" Uma says, seeing me.

I stand there in the doorway and meet Sarah's eyes and then rub my paws together, pantomiming washing them under a stream of water.

"It's Trip," Sarah says with a laugh. "Oh my God, it's our Trip!"

I scamper to the pole where they are tied, but Uma actually flinches away when I reach for her bonds.

"Are you kidding me?" Uma says. "You recognize a raccoon just like that?"

I reach for Sarah's ropes instead, pulling them with my paws and then applying my teeth.

"He loves to wash his hands like that," Sarah says. "Sometimes I think he does it just to make me laugh."

I do sometimes wash my hands in front of her just to hear her laugh, she's right. It seems like a million years ago. I chew through her ropes first, enough that she can wiggle her hands out, and then I set to Uma's.

Sarah is pulling at the ropes around her ankles, but she asks me, "You followed us all the way here, Trip?"

I nod around the ropes in my mouth, my brain working overtime on how to explain that I need her help to free the raccoons.

"Why? Why would he follow us all the way here?"

Uma asks, as I bite through the last of the ropes holding her.

That's when the door clicks shut and we all freeze in
place.

"You're back already?" Diana says loudly enough for
us to hear through the closed door.

From my immobile position I hear two voices respond.
Oh no. Moose and Zach are back.

"What's going on?" Uma whispers to Sarah.

"Shhh!" I hiss at the women.

"Did that raccoon just shush me?"

"Shhh!" says Sarah.

"Why are you yelling?" a voice I recognize as Moose's
asks, the suspicion obvious in his tone, even through
this door.

"I'm not yelling," Diana says. "I just thought you'd
be at the … at the east fence."

"Why?"

"Oh, I just saw all the humans go that way, so I
thought something might be going on," Diana says
loudly for our benefit I am sure. She's protecting us. Trying to get the other dogs to leave. I'm not just a coward,
now I'm also a jerk. A total jerk-wad. This dog is a friend
despite everything and I left her out there to deal with
a pair of bullies by herself.

"Sarah, help me," Uma whispers, and I turn to see
my brilliant humans moving furniture into the middle of

the room and climbing to reach the skylight.

"Maybe we should go to the east fence, Moose," I hear Zach say, just as Uma pushes the skylight open with a rusty creak.

"What was that?" demands Zach.

"What?" says Diana loudly as Uma scrambles up through the skylight.

"Come on, Trip," Sarah says, grabbing me around the waist and following Uma up on top of the furniture and out through the skylight on the roof.

"That lock is open!" Moose exclaims, and that's when the sounds outside sharpen into growls and barks filled with threats.

"Diana," I whisper, crawling to the edge of the roof to look down at the corgi, who is rolling in the dirt fighting with the two huge dogs. She's scrappy, but there's no way she can hold her own against the larger animals.

"What do I do, what do I do?" I repeat, pulling on my whiskers frantically, looking for something, anything to help her. That's when Pal dive-bombs into the middle of the fray. The dogs flinch away, howling, and I have no idea what's got them so freaked out until I see Malone hanging upside down by his hind paws from the owl's talons, hurling spines at the dogs with his little pink paws like they're guided missiles.

Diana drags herself away from the other dogs, her back leg looking pretty scratched up. Sarah and Uma are crouched beside me on the roof, staring goggle-eyed at the crazy mammal show below. Diana looks up at me desperately and I yell up at Pal. "Help her!"

I don't know what I expected, since the owl is already carrying a hedgehog, but he tries to circle back and runs into a tree trunk with a thud. I pull off my fanny pack, lowering it over the side of the roof. "Diana, grab it!"

She takes a panting second to understand and then reaches up with her paw, but the fanny pack isn't long enough. This is crazy. I can't let Diana die down there. I pull the fanny back up, and hand my tail to Sarah, pressing it into her hands. The human looks at me entirely confused, so I point at my tail in the palm of her hand, and I jump off the roof.

I don't know that she's understood my plan until I stop my downward descent to what would have been a truly amazing face-plant, even by my practiced stan-dards. I'm hanging by my tail, my arms extended with one end of the belt of my fanny pack hanging a half foot from the ground. "Diana! Try again!"

Diana reaches out again, and this time manages to grab the fanny pack belt and our chain of corgi, fanny pack, and raccoon are raised up towards the roof of the building by Sarah as she grips my tail. It's a painful way to travel, and I may never be able to bend my tail the way I used to after this, but somehow it works, and we are all lying on the roof puffing as two crazed dogs run around below us, howling about the hedgehog spines in their faces.

"We have to get out of here, Sarah," Uma says, pulling on her friend's arm. Her alarm is appropriate as we can see humans from this camp converging on the howling dogs from all sides.

"Diana, are you okay?" I ask, rolling over to face the dog.

"I think so," she answers, still panting. "But we won't be for long."

Sarah is still staring down at me in wonder, running her hands over my tail, as Pal comes in for one of his ungainly landings, still carrying the hedgehog. They roll to a stop right in front of Uma, who takes one look at them, shakes her head like she can't handle this and throws her jacket over the fence closest to her.

"They're going to rob our camp," Sarah says, finding her voice and directing these words at me. "They're not traders at all. Duke's people took away that raft and hid it because they didn't want us here."

"We have to run," Uma says, one leg already over the fence. We can hear the other humans trying to restrain the dogs, and we're moments away from them noticing the padlock is open. "We have to get back to our camp and warn them. Duke knows where it is and he could lead an attack back."

"Trip?" Sarah asks, getting ready to follow Uma.

I look from Diana to Pal and Malone and shake my head. I can't leave, but I recognize that Sarah and Uma's departure might help us free the raccoons.

"Sarah!" Uma hisses from over the fence.

Sarah cracks her knuckles, like she does when she's thinking hard. "This is about the raccoons Duke was talking about, isn't it? Be careful. I'll see you back at the camp, and if you don't come back, I'm coming looking for you."

I'm stunned that she understands, but she squeezes my paw before I can even think of an appropriate answer, and then she's over the fence and gone.

Diana's pulling on my other paw. "Come on, we have to get off this roof."

Helping Diana carefully, we move onto the next roof over just as the humans raise the alarm, discovering that Sarah and Uma are no longer tied up where they left them.

This is the one time I'm very happy adult humans don't understand animal speech because Moose and Zach are howling every detail of our journey to their humans as loud as they can, following us from the ground.

"Get down here you beasts!" Moose calls. "Ow!"

"Diana, you're a traitor to our camp!" Zach yells. "Ouchie!"

"Don't listen to them," I advise my corgi friend, pulling her along till we're atop the building holding the raccoons. Diana is either in too much pain to answer them, or she's distraught from her choice to help us instead of her camp, I can't tell.

"Trip!"

I turn to see two cats I know halfway up a fir tree right next to the raccoon building.

"Ginger, thank the Gods of the Garbage Dump," I say, grinning at the orange cat as he gives me a saucy wave from his branch.

"Wait, is that a dog?" Ginger asks, seeing Diana beside me, his back arching in response.

Diana stiffens, her ears flattening, but I quickly say, "She saved my life."

"Och, let me see that leg, lassie," offers Malone, coming around to look at Diana's leg as she sniffs away more tears. "No more crying now, we'll get you fixed up right fast."

Ginger still looks unconvinced, but Sonar takes a few steps in front of him, eyeing the distance between this roof and her branch, before squeezing down into a squat and launching herself at the rooftop. Pal catches her as she lands, and she laughs, hugging him close before remembering she's on a mission.

"Corporal Sonar reporting for duty," she says, saluting smartly. Ginger lands right beside her without skidding and walks over, his back only slightly arched, his eyes glued to the dog beside me.

"Here we thought we'd be rescuing you, and a dog beat us to it," he says, giving me a cat head-butt.

We're all so happy to see each other that we start talking at once, filling each other in on our various solo adventures. I'm even eager to hear Malone's long-winded tale, but first, we have to rescue some friends.

"Diana, you already know Pal." Pal gives a feathered wave. "This is Malone, Ginger, and Corporal Sonar," I say, turning to introduce the dog at my side. "These are my friends."

"Um … pleased to meet you," Diana says, her smile tremulous. She's interrupted by more insults from the dogs below.

"Get down here, traitor, before we tell on you," Zach says.

"And you better be ripping those other animals to shreds if you don't want to get thrown out of this camp to the zombies," Moose puts in.

I want to defend my friend, but it's Malone who waddles to the edge of the roof this time to call down. "Shut up, ye mangy mutts, or I'll toss a few spines into your wide behinds to match the ones on your faces."

"Yeah!" yells Sonar, running over to the edge where Malone is standing, "and I'll … I'll swipe those whiskers right off your face, I will!"

The dogs drop into stunned silence at being so severely threatened by two animals the size of their average litter droppings, and then start up the barking again, howling for their humans. Diana looks amazed at this full-throated defense, but I am not surprised. I'm just proud.

"He ran out of loose spines finishing off that zombie in the dam," Ginger explains to us, still looking curiously at Diana. "So he can't just sneeze them at mammals anymore. He has to pluck them one by one and throw them."

"Wouldn't have done any good if Sonar hadn't shown me how to throw," Malone says, still glaring down at the baying dogs on the ground. "She can hit any target that cat can."

Sonar isn't listening, though; she's walked over to the open skylight I had climbed out of. She turns horrified eyes at me, and I have to swallow a few times before I can speak. "Yes, that's a raccoon, Sonar. She was a friend. Her name was Sumi. She … died."

Ginger walks over to look down through the skylight curiously. "Um, Trip?"

"Yes?"

"I don't know who you're talking about, but that raccoon down there is alive and he's pretty angry at being chained up down there."

Sarah and Uma's escape nearly empties the camp of humans and I can only pray that they are not recaptured. It also emptied the room where they experiment on raccoons, which is probably why Winter is still tied to the metal table below and not suffering under a zombie bite.

"I don't understand," Pal says as I dig through my fanny pack for the sparkly purple shoelace we traded from the squirrels. "They have an antidote that will turn a zombie back into a regular human?"

"They're making one," I say, finding the shoelace and pulling it out. "And they're testing it on the raccoons."

"Why not test it on the zombies?" asks Malone.

"I don't know, I'm a raccoon, not a crazy human doctor. Maybe white mice are hard to find in an apocalypse," I snap, tying the shoelace to the top of the skylight.

"Trip," Sonar says and again, her voice has the power to stop me. "We're really sorry."

I sigh, trying to push down the guilt and the anger, reminding myself that these mammals came to help me. "I don't know. They capture the raccoons, they hand them to a zombie to get bitten, and then they test their antidote on the bitten raccoon."

"I think it has something to do with the time after you are bitten," Diana offers, still wincing at the pain in her leg. Malone patched it up pretty well with pieces of cloth and some tape. It's going to hurt like road rash when we pull that tape off her fur. I should know. I've been duct-taped to trees several times by the more intolerant members of my species. "Maybe there's only a little time after you are bitten by a zombie when the antidote can work."

"Whatever the reason, we have to get those raccoons out," I say, lowering the other end of the shoelace down through open skylight.

"We can't get down that way," Ginger points out, raising his padded paw. "Remember trying to cross the river? Cats don't have your raccoon dexterity. We can't grab things like ropes."

"I know," I reply. "I'll climb down and let you guys in through the door."

"I dinnae think those two beastly dogs, no offense, lassie," Malone says, "are just gonna let us traipse on in."

The shoelace dangles beside Winter now, who notices it and us through the skylight. "What are you doing back here?" he demands from his prostrate position. "Why can't you just leave?"

"Oh, he sounds like a darling, I'm so glad we're risking our lives to rescue him," Ginger says sarcastically.

"I know," I answer. "But you're the one who said we don't pick our friends based on … what was it?"

"Their usefulness," Ginger says. "But we do pick them based on whether they're friendly. Your call, Trip."

"We save them all," I say, nodding at Diana who nods back just as confidently. "Friendly or not, no animal deserves to be experimented on."

"Okay," Ginger says. "You get down there and coordinate your raccoons, we'll be ready for you by the door."

"But how?"

"Let us worry about that," Ginger says, pushing me. "Malone, you should go with Trip since you're the only other one who can climb."

Malone replies by pulling out a few more spines from his back. "Ouch, oh confounded, ouch! Here, take these, lassie," he says as he hands the spines to Sonar.

"Diana?" I ask, but she waves me away with a smile. "Get them out, I'll get your cats to the right door."

I hand her my precious fanny pack. "Here, you hold on to this until I see you again."

I think giving Diana my fanny pack is what finally convinces Ginger just how much I trust this dog. He approaches her, sniffs at her face and whiskers, and then slides along the left side of her body, scenting her. She holds still for the whole operation, which I appreciate, because it must be super weird for a dog to be scented by a cat.

"Well, at least she has the fashion sense to match me," says Ginger, finishing his scenting work and posing next to her. That makes Diana grin.

And with that we're climbing down the sparkly purple

shoelace, down to where Winter is alternating between cursing us and encouraging us.

"Careful, you're swinging," he says, critical as always. "What kind of a raccoon is that?"

"He's the hedgehog kind," I say, putting my hind paws down on the metal table finally, and holding the shoelace steady for Malone.

"Hedgehog kind?" Winter repeats doubtfully, his eyes narrowed to slits. "Don't know if I trust a raccoon with fur like that."

"Och, no one really cares, ya old coot," Malone snarks, as he slides the rest of the way down the shoelace, narrowly missing impaling us. "We're here to rescue you an' your only response needs to be thankful."

"Old coot?" Winter sputters, trying to sit up, but failing because of the chain around his neck. "Who are you calling an old coot, you ... old coot?"

"We're going to need a key for these chains," I say, ignoring both old coots, and searching the walls for a key.

"Don't bother with me," Winter says. "If you're really here on a rescue mission, go save the young ones in that room over there. Before they end up in here."

I can't argue with that logic, and Malone agrees, pulling another spine free with an "Ouch! I'll try and pick these locks. In the meantime, you get the rest of the raccoons and open that outside door for Ginger."

I bound away, making quick work of the two doors

between me and the raccoon room, and arriving out of breath.

"Trip?" says the first raccoon I pass, and then the whole room is saying my name and asking questions, but I bolt for the door that will lead to my friends, grabbing the handle with both paws.

"It's locked," Beast says from the cage beside me, and he's right.

"No," I say, wrenching at the door, and then banging on it. "Ginger! Ginger, the door is locked!"

I press my ear against the door, but I can't hear a thing. I don't know if my friends are outside ready to charge in, or if it's Moose and Zach, quietly waiting for me to make a mistake.

I run my eyes over Beast's cage, and thankfully it's got an uncomplicated locking system. A small eye hook on the outside is all that's holding him in, I pull at it until I work it free and the door swings open. He stares at it and then at me.

"Well?" I say, waving my arms like a turkey. "Help me!"

Beast jumps into action, and we run around, freeing as many raccoons as we can. We're making a huge mess with water and food spilling all over the floor, so I start assigning older raccoons to climb up and open more cages, and herd the smaller raccoons into the center of the room where they sit shivering and scared. I take one look at them and say, "You little ones, look around for a key to unlock this door."

Most of them shake their heads and bury their little masked faces, but two of the tiniest raccoon babies immediately leap out of the pack and start sniffing and looking around. I keep unlocking cages, pausing only when I get to Sumi's old cage. It's empty now, but the smell of apples and cookie dough lingers, and I grip the wire of her cage, feeling the sadness overwhelm me.

"Trip?" asks a voice behind me. I turn to see two hundred masked faces looking to me for direction. "What do we do now?"

Thankfully, it's Winter who answers, from the other door that leads back to the skylight. "This way!"

The gaze runs towards him, slipping and sliding over the floor that is slick with water and pellets of food. It's a whole pack of mammals just as clumsy as me and I can't help but smile as I follow ungracefully, picking up the smaller raccoons and handing them to others so that this jail is now just a room full of empty cages. I get to the first hallway door and slide to a stop, holding the door open for the stream of mammals awkwardly running through, and Malone holds open the other. We're like furry doorstops, calling words of encouragement until all the raccoons are in the room with the skylight. I can see Winter directing them back up the shoelace in a long line of striped tails.

I turn my face back to the room with the now empty cages to see Cho has opened the locked door that leads out to the camp and he's flanked by Moose and Zach.

"There he is!" shrieks Moose, hurling himself at me.

"Keep going," I yell at Malone as I allow the door I'd been holding open to shut behind me and turn to face our aggressors. Cho looks confused, standing in the doorway of the room with the cages, but his dogs look anything but confused.

"You're dead, raccoon," Zach spits at me.

"Probably," I admit, shaking from head to tail, wet with soggy food pellets stuck to my fur. "But at least my gaze is safe." I know I can only slow them down, but I intend to give those raccoons as much time to get up and out of that skylight as I can. I will not let them down the way I did Sumi. My cowardice will not kill another mammal, I swear it.

"Where the heck are all the raccoons?" Cho asks, stepping into the cage room, as if I could answer in a language he could understand. As if I would ever tell him.

"Not for long," Moose says. "After we're done with you, we'll hunt down your friends and ..."

He stops mid-threat, sniffing the air suddenly. Zach mimics him, but I don't need to sniff at all, I can see what's got Moose's attention: it's about six feet tall, dead, and groaning its way into the caged room.

Cho whips around at the groaning sound and screams, scrambling away, sliding on the slick floor. I freeze in place, but my eyes are still moving, and through the zombie's staggering legs, I see my friends, Ginger, Sonar, and Diana, waving at me frantically. Are they waving me towards them? Are they nuts?

Zach and Moose are losing their minds now, barking at the zombie threat but trying to stay out of his deadly reach, and Cho seems to have forgotten all about me as he searches for something to defend himself with, throwing down cages in front of the zombie.

"Trip!" Ginger calls from outside the building.

"Run!" yells Diana, the chain around her neck taut and tied to the doorknob.

"Don't think!" squeaks Sonar, jumping up and down in place.

That I can do. I run around Cho, dodging the dogs, and sprint straight at my friends. The zombie is slouching toward me, but I throw myself to the ground and slide right through his legs, as if I'm aiming for home base after a fly ball, the water all over the floor giving me enough speed to launch into the air as I hit the door's threshold.

I tumble straight into Ginger, who has his arms wide to catch me, and we turn to see Diana pull the door closed with her chain, trapping the zombie inside with Cho and his dogs.

"That should slow them down," she announces. "Now, can someone get this chain off me, please?"

I start laughing, squeezing Ginger in one arm and Pal and Sonar in the other as Malone and all the raccoons on the roof lean over the edge to see what is going on.

# CHAPTER SIXTEEN

"We have to keep moving," Ginger says to me as we walk at ground level.

"We have to find somewhere to rest," corrects Malone, waddling by. "These raccoons cannae keep walking like this. They're nocturnal, don't you know?"

I roll my eyes at him hedgehog-splaining my own sleep schedule, but Winter stops him for me. "He knows! He's a raccoon, for compost's sake. Let me tell you about this time I fell asleep waiting for a bus to move away from an abandoned lunch bag ..."

They trundle by, Winter and Malone, a skinny old raccoon who smells like tobacco and a loudmouth hedgehog with a bald spot, arguing the whole way.

"They're like an old married human couple," Ginger snickers at me.

"But they're not wrong," I answer, looking up at the trees where hundreds of raccoons negotiate their way in the relative safety of the branches. We partnered them up so no raccoon gets left behind and Beast is doing his best to shepherd the slowest ones, but he looks wiped as well. I'm walking on the ground because corgis can't climb trees on the best of days, and with her leg all scratched up, Diana's moving the slowest of all of us, and keeps apologizing for it.

"I can catch up, Trip," she says for at least the third time since we set out. "Just leave markers along the way ..."

"Even if I have to send everyone else ahead, Diana, I will not leave another friend behind," I say, running my paw over the fur on her back. I know what it feels like to be the slowest mammal in a fellowship. She smiles at me through her pain and then stops walking and sniffs curiously around us.

"Garbage can coming up," she says, her nose stuck high in the air.

About twenty trees later I stop at the garbage can secured to a tree, and with Ginger and Diana's assurances that they will scream at the top of their lungs if anyone tries to raccoon-nap me again, I crawl in, tossing edible items over my shoulders to the mammals below.

"Raisins," I yell, throwing a half-eaten box over my shoulder.

Pal swoops by with good news, reporting an abandoned mine not far away, and we find new strength in that.

Sonar encourages the youngest of the gaze to keep up the march until we arrive at the mouth of the mine. I think Wally should be very proud of his corporal, she sounds just like him. Actually, that's going to make camp life a little dodgy with two of them giving orders.

"Do you think it's safe?" I ask Ginger as we come within sight of the mine.

"Let me give it a sniff," Diana says, wincing as she walks the last few steps to the opening.

"Trip," Sonar says, walking over to me, a tiny raccoon on her back, clutching at her fur. "We can go find some food while you all sleep."

I am about to turn her down when a jaw-cracking yawn rumbles up and through my open mouth.

"Good answer," Ginger says with a grin, clapping me on the shoulder.

"It's moldy and damp, but I don't smell any other mammals," Diana calls from the mine's entrance.

It takes less than a half hour to install all the raccoons in furry piles within the safety of the mine. We do our best to cover the rocky floors in leaves and plant life to make it a bit more like a burrow, but this gaze is so exhausted from walking that they'd probably fall asleep standing on their heads at this point. We tuck Pal in as well, and his hoot-purrs lull everyone deeper into their dreams.

I make my bed at the entrance of the mine, behind

some logs, right next to Diana, whom we've managed to convince to take a break and not go hunting. I, for one, am thrilled not to be leading an expedition.

"I'm a dog," she says grumpily, licking at her leg. "I'm the best hunter you have. What do those cats knows about hunting?"

"Those cats been hunting for their own food for a long time too, Diana," I reply, not even opening my eyes. "I know this cat-dog feud was a thing before the zombies came, but you've got to let it go. I mean, I've let go of the fact that for most of my life, dogs were the enemy. We're all a few bites away from dead human food now. It's time to put that stuff aside and admit cats might have a few skills of their own. Especially *these* cats."

She snuffles in response, and I smile. I can't wait to introduce her to Emmy. If she thinks cats should hang back behind dogs, wait till she meets my mad hamster.

"Besides," I say, feeling the sun warm my back. "Who else will raise the alarm if we're attacked? You're the best guard dog I know!"

# CHAPTER SEVENTEEN

"Trip!"

"Mmm?"

"Trip, wake up. Please wake up," Diana's voice calls me out of a deep sleep.

I blink my bleary eyes open with difficulty. "What?"

"Zombies."

That word gets you moving like a jet of cold water shot at you from a garden hose. I spring up. "Where are you?" I hiss.

"Over here," she calls.

I carefully step around the wood piled up at the entrance to the mine to join her. Her long snout is in the air.

"How far away?" I ask, not even tempted to run for the trees this time, and a little surprised at my reaction. I have a whole gaze of raccoons to protect, not to mention a sleeping owl, a tired hedgehog, and an injured corgi.

"At least half an hour, if not more," she replies.

"You can smell a zombie from that far away?" I ask, surprised.

"Yup."

"Can all dogs do that?"

"Moose and Zach couldn't," she replies, a hint of pride in her voice, but it's tinged with worry.

"They might not come towards us, but if they do …"

"They're not coming this way," Diana interrupts me.

"Oh, then … why …?"

"I think Ginger and your friends are in trouble," she says, turning worried eyes towards me.

"You have to protect the gaze," I say, strapping on my fanny pack.

Winter and Malone are wearing matching looks of disagreement, but it's Malone who speaks first. "This is ridiculous, laddie. You'll need all the able bodies you have."

"And what about the less-able bodies?" I ask, pointing at the still-sleeping bundles of raccoons. "Most of those raccoons are half-starved and out of shape and the others are kits too young to fight zombies."

"But your canine friend here is injured," Winter says, pointing at Diana's leg. "She can stay behind and …"

"It's scabbed over," Diana replies defensively, flexing her leg to show us.

"I need her nose," I answer, backing Diana up. "And Pal is going to scout ahead and see if he can find help." I pat the owl on the back as he hastily swallows down a few bugs. This adventure is going to give us all a monumental case of indigestion.

"The whippersnapper's not listening," Winter says to Malone with a grimace.

"He never does," Malone answers, twirling a spine between his little pink digits. "Why, the first time I met him ..."

Diana, Pal, and I start to back away from the pair slowly, instinctively sensing this is our moment to escape.

I look at the sleeping gaze in the cave as we get some distance. "Let's hope they actually notice if someone attacks. Those two could argue through a garbage truck backing into them."

"Or a zombie apocalypse?" Pal hoots back softly.

"Exactly," I say. "Pal, you can fly faster than we can run, I'll call up Diana's olfactory directions."

Pal leaps into the air, flapping his wings in his ungainly fashion, as I climb the nearest tree so I can keep an eye on Pal while Diana hobbles on the ground at the best speed she can muster.

"Veer left," she puffs from below, the pain still audible in her voice.

"Stop as much as you need to, Diana," I call down to her, my worry for her about equal to my worry for

Ginger and his troop. The truth is, those cats really can handle themselves in most zombie situations.

"See anything yet?" I call up through the branches to Pal.

"Not since the last time you asked me," Pal hoots back, his deep voice resonating around us.

I jump through two leafy branches instead of landing on them, and fall straight through to the forest floor, hitting the ground ahead of Diana with a thump.

"I'm fine," I say, dusting myself off and climbing the next tree. This goes on for longer than I'd care to admit. And by "this" I mean this speedy scramble through the trees punctuated by even speedier plunges down to the ground and then a resumption of the scramble. Diana is a kind animal, though, and says nothing no matter how many times I scare her with my acrobatics.

"Coming up on the river," Pal calls, as I hit the ground again and decide to stay there for a while, if only to give my tail-end a few less bruises. I have a moment to hope Mrs. King is close by to give me a quick lift across before Diana calls from behind me.

"Wait, Trip!"

I skid to a stop at the end of the trees lining the beach. It looks like a war zone. The dam is in pieces and zombies roam all around on both beaches, this side and that. I scramble behind the nearest tree, casting my eyes around for signs of beavers. My heart thumps loudly in my ears. They made it out. They have to have made it out.

"No, no," I whisper, as Diana catches up to me.

"What happened?" she gasps, looking at all the zombies, her ears flattened against her head, her entire body vibrating.

Pal is already doing a wide circle over the river, his eyes wide and concerned. The only indication that there even was a dam to begin with is the lingering shape of the edges, two small stumps that extend to the sandy beach on either side, but the middle is totally gone. The logs and daubing and even the zombie we killed, all gone, swept away out of sight downstream.

"Can you climb?" I whisper to the dog as a zombie passes just in front of us.

"I have to," she replies, putting her two front paws on the tree trunk. I push her up from the bottom as she digs her claws into the bark. We struggle, but finally manage to get her up and onto the first branch. It's only about the length of her body off the ground, but it makes us both feel a little safer. Which isn't much.

Suddenly, Pal swoops down low over the far side of what's left of the dam, skimming the surface of the water.

"Careful," I whisper, pulling at my whiskers as the zombies wave their arms at Pal.

"What is he doing?" Diana whispers at me, her breath tickling my ear.

Pal passes over the spot twice more before gliding over to us in the tree.

"They're all in there," he exclaims, out of breath from dodging zombies, and landing perfectly on my branch for the first time in our friendship.

"They're in that little stump of the dam?" I ask, squinting at the broken edge, trying to see them. "All the kits and Mrs. King?"

"No, all of them," Pal explains as he flicks water off his feathers. "Ginger, Sonar, and all the beavers."

"Great galloping garburators," I say, yanking a whisker free and automatically tucking it into my fanny pack before returning to pulling on my whiskers. At this rate of constant stress, my face will be as smooth as a freshly shaved human soon.

"I couldn't get a straight answer as to what happened," he says, flapping the water off his wings. "But they were saying something about Duke and his humans."

"Why doesn't that surprise me?" I say, shaking as I look at the zombies below. "There are so many zombies, though. Why are there so many of them?"

"I recognize them," Diana exclaims.

"You what?"

"That one, over there, she was at my camp," she says, pointing her nose in the direction of a blond zombie wading through the river. "She used to kick me awake in the mornings. And those two men on the far side of the bank, they were from my camp too. Oh, and this one closest to us. Trip, half these zombies are from my camp!"

"New zombies, wonderful," I say, unsurprised by this development, and I will admit, a little happy that the humans who had mistreated Diana and killed Sumi were now mindless monsters. As my old gaze-mate Ariana would have said, karma's an itch. I think she meant that it was annoying.

"How do we get them out?" Pal asks.

"How do you get who out?" a voice above us asks.

I somehow manage not to fall out of the tree in surprise, whipping around to see the same glamorous squirrel I met on the other side of the river. The one who lost his peanut butter when I dropped his nuts. His tail fur is still distractingly glamorous, but I shake my head to focus. "How did you get over here?"

"Over where?" he replies, throwing an empty nutshell over his shoulder.

"Over here, on this side of the river," I ask.

"Who is this?" hoots Pal.

"RuPeter," the squirrel answers, with a flick of his fabulous tail. "And you're standing in the south wing of my home."

"You mean RuPaul," Diana corrects.

"No, RuPeter," he answers with a frown. "Who's RuPaul?"

Pal opens his mouth and closes it, amazed into silence,

but I have dealt with fancy animals before. I unzip my fanny pack and dig through, pulling out the sparkly purple shoelace I know is in there.

RuPeter's eyes grow to double their size as he looks at the shiny thing in my paws.

"Now, how. Did. You. Get. Across?" I ask, waving the shoelace teasingly.

"With my bone boat," the mesmerized squirrel replies, his eyes locked on the shoelace.

The bone boat as it turns out is a hollowed-out log about two feet long with crisscrossed bones laid over the top acting as a type of latticed roof. No, I'm not kidding. Yes, it is as creepy as it sounds.

"Where … what … who?" poor Pal can't even articulate the questions bouncing around his head as he hops around this odd conveyance.

The squirrel runs his paw over the bones with pride and I concentrate on not shuddering. Around RuPeter's neck, tied in a flamboyant bow, is the sparkly shoelace I've traded for this one-way trip to the other side of the river with a stop at the dam where my friends are trapped.

"The hollow log was simple enough to find with all the beavers in residence, but the bones I tied to the top act as camouflage. The zombies think it's a dead … thing," he explains.

"But why would you build it at all?" Diana asks.

"I'm the only transport vessel on this river," the squirrel says proudly. "Nest supplies, foraged items, foodstuffs, you name it, I've carried it across in my boat."

"What about mammals?" I ask, stepping into the boat and finding it surprisingly stable. Of course, this was on dry land, nestled on the forest floor. Diana follows me in and the boat creaks in protest.

RuPeter scratches his chin before answering. "Don't see why not. If the mammals were on the smaller side." He looks me up and down as if measuring my buoyancy. I suck in my gut in response and Diana tries to look as lean as a sausage-shaped dog can.

"Never mind," she says, backing out. "I'm a great swimmer; I don't need a boat."

"The problem isn't the swimming, it's the zombies," says RuPeter, twirling his new sparkly tie. "Remember all those beavers I was talking about?"

"Mr. King," I mumble, remembering what Mrs. King said about losing her mate.

"This is the most dangerous part," RuPeter announces cheerfully in front of me. We've got the log hoisted above our shoulders, pointed toward the beach, bone roof facing up. "Hopefully your owl friend can draw some attention away from us."

I can't see Pal, but I can hear him screeching like he's a conspiracy of ravens rather than a single small bird. Hopefully he's drawing undead attention from a tree branch, safely on the other side of the river, as we discussed.

"All the zombies are gathered at the base of Pal's tree," RuPeter reports. "They're gnashing their teeth at him, but none of them are trying to climb the tree."

It sounds as though Pal is the safest member of our troop by far. Slowly, the zombies on this side take notice of his screeches, turning to slouch their way through the river.

"Now?" Diana whispers from behind me somewhere. I can't look back at her because I'm carrying a boat, but I shake my head carefully.

"Be patient," I whisper, watching the zombies closest to me. Another two drift into the river, slogging through the water.

"Trip!"

"Not yet!"

"No, look!" Diana says more loudly now.

Her voice is all high and scared, so I lift the boat even higher, to see what's got her so freaked out, and I see Ginger hanging over the side of the destroyed dam, his paws in the water. You know things are bad when a cat is willingly sticking his paws in water.

"Go!" I yell at RuPeter, and we start running for the beach, the boat bumping our heads with every step. Diana is right behind us, and we drop the boat into the water, hoping against hope that the splash doesn't draw unwanted undead attention. RuPeter climbs in deftly and I give the boat a push before scrambling in right behind him with far less grace. I look up through the lattice of bones and shudder.

This squirrel's ingenuity extends far beyond fabulous hair care to inserting small flat bones through the sides of the log, high enough to use as oars but not let water in. I grab one of these bone oars and start pushing.

"Not like that," RuPeter hisses at me. "Haven't you ever rowed before?"

"Shockingly, no," I hiss back.

The boat rocks suddenly to our right, and I let out a squeal of fright before hearing Diana's voice from outside the boat.

"You're veering off course," she says, explaining the push we just got. "I'm pushing you in the right direction."

"Be careful," I whisper, seeing a pair of human legs through the lattice bones of our roof.

"Help me," grunts RuPeter, at the oars. His magnificent tail is getting wet on the floor of our boat, which draws my attention to the water that is seeping in. I can feel the terror rising in my throat, but I grab a bone oar and try to mimic the squirrel's movements. This goes on for an interminable amount of time. It couldn't have been more than five minutes, but it feels like days, and the muscles in my shoulders are screaming almost as loud as the garbage truck that used to careen around the corner of my burrow on Thursday mornings. That garbage man loved his death metal. I can't see out the front of the boat, because there's a squirrel madly rowing in front of me, so the only way I can measure our progress across the river is that Pal's voice is getting louder in my ears. We get another nudge from Diana, the rocking motion bringing in even more water. We're now haunch deep in river water. I don't know how much longer I can do this.

"I'm going to help Pal," Diana announces. "You're really close to the dam, Trip, good luck."

"No, Diana!" I call out, sick to my stomach at the idea of her dodging twenty zombies on dry land. I swallow back a scream as my yell draws the attention of a zombie I hadn't seen before, leaning over our boat and peering through the lattice with his milky eyes. Actually, my voice is stolen from me because I know that bald pate.

"Heave ho, I see the dam," RuPeter announces as if this were a perfectly normal voyage, steering us toward it by leaning heavily on his bone oar.

The zombie who was once named Duke seems to have been fooled by the bones atop our boat, and turns his terrifying face to the shore, where I can hear Diana barking.

"Please be okay," I whisper up to the Gods of the Garbage, but my prayer is interrupted by a loud thump.

RuPeter scampers to the helm, and throws a large

stone tied around a rope over the side of our bone boat. This squirrel is nothing if not efficient. I run right past him to see Ginger, soaking wet, his paws wrapped tightly around two kits.

"Finally," he says, passing me little Olivia King. "I was out of ideas and Mrs. King ...," he looks down at the other kit in his paws. "She will be right back, I'm sure."

Olivia is already crying, so I suspect Mrs. King has been gone for longer than is safe, but I reach for her brother Alec, placing him beside his sister in the boat. Once we have all the kits, I raise my arms to help Sonar board, but RuPeter shakes his head at me. "Too much weight," he announces.

"Then you take Sonar and the kits," I say, climbing up and into the ruined dam so that I'm beside Ginger. "I'll wait here till you get back."

"But ...." Sonar opens her mouth to argue, but then Hetty King starts wailing and she immediately turns to hug her close. "Roger that, I will keep the kits safe until Mrs. King gets back."

"I'll take them downstream," RuPeter says. "Somewhere safe. Send your owl after us."

I nod to the squirrel, who hauls up the stone anchor and starts instructing Sonar on the use of the oars. I wrap my arms around Ginger. He leans into me, releasing all the tension in his wiry body. We sit there, watching as the boat pulls away, and then we back further into the dam as a pair of zombies slosh their way through the river right next to us.

"You can just barely see Pal through this hole in the dam," Ginger whispers, pointing up at a spot where the branches of the dam are not as dense. Sure enough, when I stick my eye into the hole I can see Pal dancing from claw to claw. He's getting hoarse, but I can hear Diana quite clearly, her barks continuing to pull the attention of the zombies. I wish I could see her, but I can at least console myself with the confident and loud sound of her voice.

"Do you smell …." I trade my eye for my nose, sticking it up through the hole in the dam, "… smoke?"

Ginger sniffs the air, and his eyes go wide, his ears flattening. "Trip," he hisses, pulling on my tail. I turn to see a zombie arm reaching into the dam. We press ourselves against the only remaining wall in the structure, and Ginger wraps an arm against my gut, pushing it in like a corset.

"Hold on," I hear Diana say from somewhere behind us, and I have a moment to wonder how in the world she can help us when I hear the sound of a hamster in triumph. Just in case you're wondering what that sounds like, it's a long wavering high-pitched trill. Basically, imagine a wolf howl after the wolf has breathed in a lot of helium.

Ginger and I look at each other in the confines of this destroyed dam and whisper, "Emmy!"

The zombie hesitates, retracting his arm — to see what the hubbub is about, I'm sure — and then he's sloshing away from us, heading upstream.

We carefully edge our way back to the end of this stub of a dam and I swear, there's not a zombie to be seen in the river or on the beach we just came from. The noises ahead of us are loud and crackling, and the smell is putrid and smoky.

Of course, it's my curious cat friend who climbs out of the dam and onto it first, his tail hanging down in my face so that I have to call up. "What's going on up there?"

"Come up and see," he says, his tail switching rapidly. From my limited translation abilities in cat tail communication, I think he's excited.

I grab the edge of the dam and haul myself up to see an amazing sight. Pal, Wally, and Diana are herding zombies their way with their barks, hisses, and hoots, towards a rope strung tightly between two trees. Diana and Wally run under the rope and then veer left into a gorse bush and Pal flies right above them. They can't run straight because directly behind the rope is a huge bonfire of zombies. Under it all must be a pile of wood, but all you can see at this point are the bodies of zombies, charring and turning black. Every few minutes, Emmy streaks by at top speed, still screaming her blood-curdling scream, rounding up any zombies who might have wandered away from her road to ruin.

"They've almost got all of them," Ginger says, admiration in his voice. "Here! You!"

"What are you doing?" I gasp, as a large zombie turns his face toward us.

"Helping!" Ginger announces, leaping from the dam onto the sand and streaking in front of the zombie. I watch in amazement as he mimics Wally and Diana, hissing and caterwauling, until the zombie is pursuing him, arms outstretched, mouth gaping. He trundles after my best friend and then trips over the rope, as all his brethren did before him, landing face first in the fire. He doesn't seem to understand the issue, pushing himself back up on his elbows, the flames covering his body not disturbing him at all, but then an impossibly heavy log drops from the trees onto his back squashing him in place.

"Take that, you beast!" yells Mrs. King from the branches of the tree as her entire brood cheers from the shore.

# CHAPTER EIGHTEEN

In all, there had to be about forty zombies on that pile, and I was happy to give one hundred percent of the credit to the small brown hamster who continues to patrol the bonfire.

"She's got a thing about fire," Wally says with a shake of his head.

"We're lucky she does," I say, grinning from ear to ear, but then losing my smile as I remember. "Hey, what are you even doing here? I thought you'd be back at the camp organizing the defenses — don't tell me Uma and Sarah haven't made it back yet?"

Wally gives the star on his collar a polish before answering. "Uma and Sarah got back in plenty of time, and most of Duke's camp never made it, as you can see, they ran into a pack of zombies and weren't as clever as our Emmy. The rest are still limping back this way. Our humans routed them with ease."

Emmy passes us again on her circle, casting a curious eye at the dog beside me before continuing her patrol.

"So, everyone is all right?" Ginger presses.

"Every mammal is safe and accounted for back home," Wally says, "which is why Emmy and I felt comfortable enough to lead this counterattack."

"You're looking a little on the skinny side, my raccoon friend," he says, poking my tummy like it's morning inspection. "How did your own quest proceed?"

I look back at the sandy beach, where another group of bewildered raccoons are unloading from the bone boat, closely followed by Mrs. King and her kits.

"Nearly perfectly," I answer, remembering the smell of apples and cookie dough. "But these raccoons will need time to recover from captivity."

We were lucky that Mrs. King and RuPeter formed a partnership for the use of this river, because otherwise I don't know how I would have transported the rescued raccoons.

"This way," Sonar instructs the raccoons, leading them to the bonfire to warm up.

"Sonar was amazing," I say to Wally. "At first I couldn't believe you sent her to help us, but now I see why."

Wally snorts in response. "I didn't send that kitten out to join you! I sent her to deliver your blessed fanny pack and return to the camp."

"I knew it!" declares Ginger, smacking a paw on the ground.

"She went AWOL, and for that, she must be disciplined," says Wally. "I'll have to demote her to a private."

"Wally, you can't do that," I say, lowering my voice so the kitten in question won't overhear us. "It will destroy her."

"She has to learn!" he barks back at me, the drill sergeant in him rising to the surface, his chest sticking out at my questioning his orders.

Emmy skids to a stop next to us. "She's a hero!"

It's a sight I've missed, Emmy, in all her tiny glory, standing on her two back paws, glaring up at Wally, who has literally coughed up hair balls bigger than her.

"If you don't promote Sonar," she says, poking Wally's bronze star with her little finger, "I'll find an even huger star for her to wear, and we'll start our own squadron!"

Wally gapes at the small hamster, but she turns away from him, like that decision has been made. She takes another look at Diana, who looks uncomfortable under the hamster's gaze, and then Emmy takes off on her patrol again.

"Has Emmy seen a dog since she lost her partners to zombies?" Ginger asks out of the side of his mouth.

"Don't think so," I reply, wondering if that means Emmy will take Diana under her wing, or if she will avoid the dog because of bad memories. I remind myself to tell Diana about Emmy's origin story. It's a big part of why I was able to trust Diana after all, despite my previous canine experiences.

"That's the last of them," Pal announces, coming in for a tumbling landing. Sure enough, riding on Mrs. King's wide tail, we see Winter and Malone, a heated argument between them as they get to the beach. RuPeter is a few oar strokes behind her, carrying the last of the raccoons.

"I told you not to touch it, the spines grow back very quick," Malone says angrily, jumping off Mrs. King's tail, and waddling into the water to help raccoons disembark the bone boat.

"Are you sure you're a raccoon?" demands Winter, sucking on a finger and following Malone off the boat.

"For the last time you limey mammal, I am a hedgehog!" Malone yells back at Winter.

"Never heard of 'em," Winter mumbles under his breath.

Mrs. King shakes the water off her body. "That's everyone. Phew!"

I look around at all the animals and put two fingers between my teeth to give a whistle. "We should stay here tonight, rest up, and then we can head back to our camp in the morning. Mrs. King, you should pack the bare essentials from your home."

Two hundred masked faces, six beavers and a hedgehog

look around at each other and then back at me, with guilty looks.

"Ah, laddie, we should tell you what we decided on the trip over," Malone says, tracking slowly towards me.

"What?" I say, worry beginning to gnaw at me anew. "What do you mean?"

Malone gestures for Winter to explain, sitting down on the sand and crossing his pink paws.

"Fine. I'll be the bad guy. We've decided to stay here," Winter says. "With Mrs. King."

"What?" I say, actually taking a step back from Winter and bumping into Ginger. They can't be serious. I just found them!

"Mrs. King is going to need help rebuilding the dam," Malone explains, risking a glare from Winter at his interruption. "And your camp is not really set up to accommodate two hundred raccoons, is it laddie?"

"Rebuilding the dam?" I parrot. They can't be serious. "Mrs. King, surely it's not safe for you and the kits. You have to come home with us!"

"This *is* our home, Trip," Mrs. King replies, gathering her kits close. "We live in rivers, not on land. We can't just pick up and move into a human camp. Where would we get food? And how would we get around? You see how slow we are on land."

I glance at Wally, Ginger, and Emmy for support, but they're listening to this argument like they're open to the idea. Which is crazy. Isn't it? "Sure, we might have to expand … maybe look for a stream that has fish nearby."

"Beavers don't live in streams and we're not housecats," Winter says, looking around at the gaze of raccoons, who are all nodding at him. "These trees on this side of the river are thick and heavy with spots for burrows. Especially with fall coming on, and the hibernation schedule."

"I … but …." I can feel my throat closing up at the thought of being alone again. "What about the zombies?"

Little Hetty King gives a squeak of fear and I realize how Pickles felt that day we went for a walk and talked about home. Home is different for every mammal. And for these mammals, this feels like home.

"We'll watch out for each other," RuPeter says, giving his bone boat a pat. "All of us. And your hedgehog Malone and I were talking about setting up a tree-to-tree highway to get from this river all the way to your camp. Could open up a whole new trade route for me. I mean, for *us*, Mrs. King."

"You'd stay too, Malone?" Sonar asks, speaking up for the first time in the conversation.

"Ah lassie," Malone answers, the regret heavy in his voice. "I think I must. I'm too old to take on a new human pet. Too much responsibility. But this is a project I can see through to the end. Rebuilding the dam. Getting this gaze established."

"Maybe I should stay too," Sonar says, hesitantly, looking sideways at Wally for approval, her tail sketching "S" shapes of insecurity in the sand.

Emmy bumps Wally from behind, and the older cat harrumphs and then says, "A contingent out here on the boundaries would be a strategic advantage. But I couldn't leave a corporal in charge."

Sonar hangs her head dejectedly, and Diana glares at Wally. She looks a little like Emmy when she does that.

"I'd have to promote you to sergeant," Wally says, raising his chin impossibly high.

Sonar's head comes up so fast I hear pops in her neck. "Really?"

"It's the only thing to do," Wally says, standing tall. "Sergeant Sonar, will you hold this position?"

Sonar salutes smartly, clicking the heels of her back paws together. "Aye, General!"

Malone grins widely, but then turns his face to me, "Well laddie, what about you?"

"What about me?" I ask, my voice heavy with sadness. Doesn't anyone care that I'll be alone again?

"Are you gonna stay with us?" he says, looking around at the raccoons. "With your gaze?"

I cast my eyes around at all the encouraging faces, and then turn to look at the rest of my friends who stand apart from the gaze, locking eyes with Diana last.

"You know I'd stay and help," Diana says apologetically. "But I'm a dog. I can't live in a tree."

"Of course not," says Mrs. King. "We're so blessed the raccoons are staying, we couldn't ask you to stay as well."

Now Diana is staring at me. "I would understand if you decided to stay, Trip, and maybe your friends would introduce me to a new pet back at your camp?"

"Of course we would," Ginger says, sitting down next to Diana. "But we won't need to. Trip's coming home with us."

Emmy crosses her arms over her chest and glares at me, as if daring me to disagree.

I'm torn in half like a Twizzler.

I'm lying on my stomach in a bough of a tree, my tail wrapped around me like a scarf as I listen to the sounds of the forest. It's past midnight and after another grand meal of fresh fish, the cats are fast asleep in a small pile below my position. Diana is curled up nearby, her nose tucked under her paw. Emmy is lying perpendicular between the dog and the cats, grinding her teeth, though not as loudly as usual. You can always tell that hamster's mood by the decibel level of her grinding. Somehow the beavers are sleeping soundly in the bone boat, which is tethered to the stump of the dam. I'd have nightmares if I woke up and saw bones above me, but beavers are made of tougher stuff. Malone and Winter fell asleep mid-argument in RuPeter's northern wing, also known as a nest in this tree. Most of the raccoons are in their own trees, already building their burrows, negotiating with resident chipmunks, whispering excitedly about the future.

"So?" Pal asks for probably the third time since Malone and Winter finally shut up.

"I still don't know," I sigh at him, my eyes fixed on the animals below me.

"You did what you set out to do, Trip," he says. "You aren't the last raccoon on Earth. You found more of your kind. Lots more."

"I know," I say. "But is it my destiny to never live with raccoons again? Am I supposed to be alone forever?"

"I told you this before you set out on this adventure," Pal says. "You have a family. It's us. Back at the camp."

"And what about this gaze?" I say, turning my head to look at him.

He hoots softly to himself and sticks his beak into his chest to pull out a feather that was bothering him, spitting it out before he answers. "Families are more than one thing, Trip. Just like home is more than one thing. You're part of our family too. We need you. And you need us."

I look down through the leaves of my bough at the sleeping animals. It makes me smile to see that Sonar is no longer clinging to Wally in her sleep.

"These raccoons are a strong gaze; they'll take care of each other and Mrs. King, and the kits," Pal says. "Maybe they'll be even better without you leading them."

"Why?"

"Because they need to find their own strength," Pal says. "The way you did when you left our camp to come out here. You've changed."

"I still feel like the same cowardly bumbling tagalong," I say before I can stop myself. They're not even my words. It's that repetitive voice in my head back again, that snake with the forked tongue.

Pal tilts his head at me, and I realize I haven't heard that doubting voice for some time. Even now, I'm digging deep into my brain to remember what he used to sound like. And I'm doubting his doubting words.

"Except you saved a whole gaze of raccoons," Pal says. "Plus a drowning kitten in a log, a browbeaten corgi, a lonely hedgehog, two captured humans, and me when I fell in the river."

"I guess ... I did," I say, seeing myself through his eyes for the first time and wondering how I had done all that. I'd never stopped to think about it. I'd just ... done it because I had to. Because I couldn't lose my family.

"Those aren't the actions of a cowardly tag-along," he says, blinking his huge eyes. "They're the work of a brave and loving friend."

"They are?"

Pal nods wisely. Actually, he's an owl, so whenever he nods he looks wise.

It's shocking to see yourself in an entirely new light, but there you have it. Pal's right. I'm not the same raccoon who followed a pair of cats on their quest to find their pets. I'm not even the same raccoon who raced after a tail desperate to find their own kind so they could feel like less of an outsider.

I feel a warmth course through me and I look back down through the leaves. I know what I have to do.

# CHAPTER NINETEEN

"We'll see you in ten days, Sergeant," says Wally, saluting Sonar.

"Yes, sir," she answers, her troop of beavers right behind her.

"Stay out of trouble, Malone," I say, giving the hedgehog a careful hug. His new spines are coming in and look like tiny, dangerous stubble. I think they'd give me a heck of a whisker burn if I brushed against them.

"Och, I'll be fine laddie," he says with a grin. "You just get your mammals home safe and start building your end of the tree-to-tree highway. You remember what I told you?"

"Build directly south so we meet in the middle and avoid the rotten wood," I repeat, surprised at how emotional I feel leaving this old coot behind.

"Don't know how he's going to be able to tell the good branches from the bad," Winter grumbles.

"I'll help him sniff it out," Diana says, sidling up to stand next to me. "Goodbye, Winter."

He gives her a nod, which is a far cry from where their relationship started, and it's enough to make Diana smile. Maybe Diana can change every mammal's mind about her species.

I pull on my fanny pack, feeling its emptiness, but looking forward to filling it anew.

"Goodbye, Trip," the voices of my gaze call down from their new homes, waving and happy.

I wave back, tears flowing freely. "I'll be back soon, I promise!"

"Come on, Trip," Wally says, leading the way. "The sooner we leave, the sooner you can come back for a visit. Between you and Sergeant Sonar, I expect a report every fortnight from this outpost."

Pal takes off ahead of us, keeping an eye on our path for zombies, and I keep glancing back over my shoulder at the branches full of raccoons until I can't see them anymore.

As usual, Emmy is circling us in a wide orbit at top hamster speed. The rest of us walk in relative silence; our eyes and ears open for both undead and alive mammals. Wally is in front, whistling some kind of marching song, in a hurry to get back to his new twin baby human charges.

I trip over a branch, turn it into a front roll, and come up on all fours again.

"You okay?" Diana asks from just ahead of me, and her concern makes me laugh. It's so funny that this adventure started with me at my very lowest, following a tail with no body, and is ending with me looking forward to the future, following a dog with no tail.

"He's fine," says Ginger from my left before I can answer.

"Not fine," says Emmy as she slows down to walk on my right. "But he will be."

"Yes, I will be," I say, walking proud amongst these animals, tailed and tail-less, clumsy and graceful, back to our camp and the rest of our family.